Praise for
3 DEAD PRINCES

"This is a beautiful book. The illustrations are wonderful. It definitely rocks! I ought to know."—**Iggy Pop**

"We need more heroines like Princess Stormy!
This is the fairy tale I've been searching for since becoming a parent over a decade ago. Complete with strength, magic and mutual aid, *3 Dead Princes* keeps the pages turning for all ages. No other tale told before it combines rich, imaginative story-telling with a theme of cooperation as an ideal and necessary base on which to rebuild society like this one does. An alternative fairy tale for anarchist/punk/fellow traveler parents to read with their kids!"

—**Jessica Mills**, author of *My Mother Wears Combat Boots: A Parenting Guide for the Rest of Us*

An E.A.P. Fairy Tale for Adults of All Ages

Also from
EXTERMINATING ANGEL PRESS

Dirk Quigby's Guide to the Afterlife
by E. E. King

Jam Today: *A Diary of Cooking
With What You've Got*
by Tod Davies

Correcting Jesus: *2000 Years of
Changing the Story*
by Brian Griffith

The Supergirls: *Fashion, Feminism,
Fantasy, and the History of
Comic Book Heroines*
by Mike Madrid

3 Dead Princes

An Anarchist Fairy Tale by

Danbert Nobacon

ILLUSTRATED BY ALEX COX

EXTERMINATING ANGEL
PRESS

Portions of this book first appeared, some in different form, on the Exterminating Angel Press online magazine at
www.exterminatingangel.com

EXTERMINATING ANGEL PRESS
"Creative Solutions for Practical Idealists"
Visit **www.exterminatingangel.com** to join the conversation
info@exterminatingangel.com

Book design by Mike Madrid
Typesetting by John Sutherland

Nobacon, Danbert, 1962-
  3 dead princes : an anarchist fairy tale / by Danbert Nobacon ;
illustrated by Alex Cox. -- 1st ed.
      p. cm.
  Summary: Princess Alexandra Stormybald Wilson, a thirteen-year-old prince killer, lives with her stepmother Queen Gwynmerelda and her father, King Walterbald, until she is initiated into the Order of the Accidental Adventurers.
  ISBN 978-1-935259-06-0 (alk. paper) -- ISBN 978-1-935259-10-7 (electronic book)
  [1. Fairy tales. 2. Kings, queens, rulers, etc.--Fiction. 3. Princesses--Fiction.] I. Title. II. Title: Three dead princes.
  PZ8.N63Aam 2010
  [Fic]--dc22
                                                          2010016249

Printed in The United States of America
Ashland, Oregon

Contents

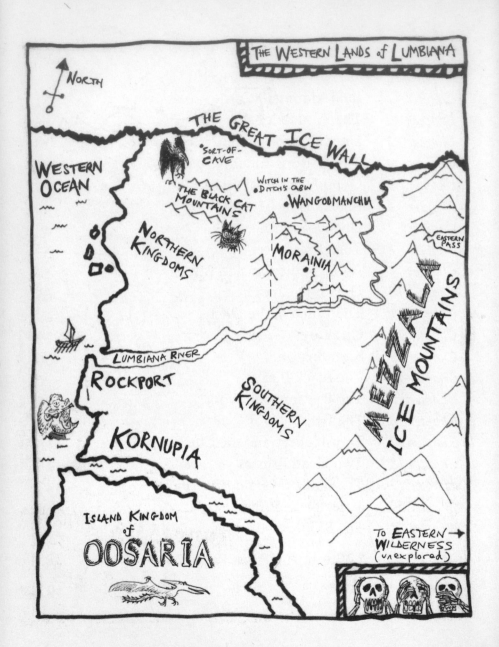

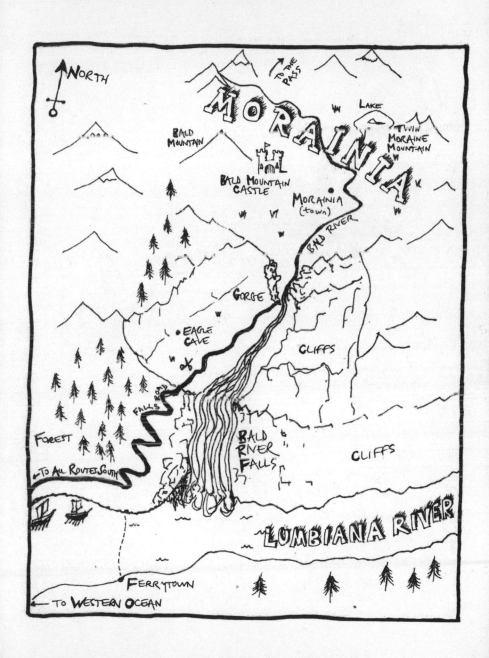

For Stella and Carson...

Prologue

Once upon a hiccup in time, there was a sort-of-fairy tale world. That is, it was as we might imagine a fairy tale world to be, with sort-of-castles and sort-of-knights riding around on sort-of-horses, occasionally stumbling upon sort-of-monsters, and people generally being in the thrall of strange magickery going on, but there was something else about it too. Something we cannot quite put our finger on.

Or as The Fool would have said:

The bird laid an egg. But I'm ahead of myself now
And in truth the black bird was a boy
Not a boy, but a boy-bird, you begin to see how
This whole world was off-kilter some …

Chapter 1
BALD MOUNTAIN CASTLE

"How? How can you? It's summer. School's out! You can't leave me with … with," she spat it out, "… *Lady Muck Batbreath*."

"Now, Alex," the King began. He always said "Now, Alex …" when he was trying to calm the tempests that whipped up inside his daughter, even though he knew that, as she got older, it was more and more like pissing in the wind.

The King was discovering, for the zillionth time, that his daughter, Princess Alexandra Stormybald Wilson, could be very Stormy indeed. Perhaps it was her age, yes, he thought, that was it. Probably the snowstorm that raged during the first moon of deep winter on the night she was born, over thirteen winters before, had little or no actual bearing on her character.

"No," Alexandra Stormy continued, "Bats are too good for *her*. She is bat vomit, after the bat has eaten rotting mosquitoes, and it's not just puke; it's coming out both ends."

King Walterbald Wilson the Second of Morainia couldn't help repressing a smile. "This is the Queen you're talking about. Such respect for your elders. Tsk, tsk."

"Don't patronize me," snarled Princess Stormy.

"Oh my. When did my daughter learn to use such big words?"

Now, the King did sound patronizing to his only child. But

1

his words had come out wrong, as they sometimes did when he tried to make a joke that, in his own boyish imagination, might make light of his daughter's woes. What he was really thinking to himself was: what a clever girl, such a fertile imagination. And then, with a tinge of sadness, so like her mother.

But his daughter didn't get it.

"Dad, you just don't get it."

"Now Alex ... You're right. I probably don't get it, but that doesn't alter the fact ..."

"The fact that you are going off gallivanting around, exploring, adventuring, and having a right royal ball, and leaving me here for two whole moons with Snot-for-Brains." And with that, she threw herself on the bed to hide the tears of rage welling up in her brown eyes.

King Walterbald sighed. "I'll be back in a few weeks. In plenty of time for Archmother Night."

"But Daaad!!"

"Alex. I ... 'er, well ..." Relenting perhaps inevitably, he gave way. "Well, I never said ... Well, all I actually said was that you can't come with me. Not this time. It's too dangerous. And, well, it was going to be a surprise, but I never said that you had to stay here, 'er, period."

Now Stormy, unusually for her, was the one struggling for words.

"What? What is it?"

"I'm not giving away any details. Suffice to say I have arranged for you to go on a trip of your own, and for some weeks, I believe. You could even call it an adventure."

"A mystery adventure? I love it. When do I go? Who's taking me, Geraldo?"

"Erm, no. Geraldo will have to stay here to keep an eye on things. 'Er ... not to ... well, after all ... The Fool ... yes, definitely The Fool ... he'll ..."

"The Fool! You're leaving me, and you're counting on The Fool to take me Zuss-knows-where? Dad, I don't believe this! The Fool couldn't organize a piss up in a potstillery!"

"Well, prepare to be surprised then," snapped the King. But seeing his daughter's face, he went and sat on the edge of her bed.

"Alex. Darling. It may come as another, not unrelated, surprise. But we adults do have an inkling of how this might be a challenging and exciting time for someone of your age. We were all young once you know, and you might want to have a little trust in our wisdom and experience, once in a while."

"But, you're a boy. I mean you were a boy."

And I still feel like one much of the time, Walterbald thought to himself, hoping that he could trust his own judgment in sending his daughter out into a world where a certain amount of danger was guaranteed.

The King exhaled a deep breath. With a heavy heart, he bent to kiss his daughter on the cheek. "Good night, darling. And I know you will not have it all your own way, but I wish you a great summer. I'll be gone before breakfast. Sweet dreams. I love you."

"I love you too, Dad," and she hugged him a hug that lasted eons. Or so it felt. Those hugs do, sometimes.

Afterwards, when her head sank deep into the pillow,

Stormy's thoughts raced ahead like clouds in a stormy sky. Beyond the town and lake and into the forest they flew, towards the snow-capped mountains and the ocean she could barely remember seeing. Her thoughts raced toward everything that lay beyond her. Feeling half scared and half excited, she imagined looking out on a vast new world of possibility—blooming like a whole mountainside of balsam root greeting the Spring.

Chapter 2
THE WONDERLOOK

On his way downstairs, Walterbald looked in on Gwynmerelda in the royal bedroom. The Queen sat up in bed reading.

"How did she take it?" she asked without looking up.

"Oh you know. It could have been worse."

"How?" snorted Gwynmerelda. This time she *did* look up.

"Well ..." And then the King faltered, finishing the thought in his head: *I could have told her the truth.*

"You're leaving us at a time like this? Why not the day after tomorrow?"

"We've been through this, love ... no time to lose, 'er ... and," (this said more sheepishly) "I, 'er, I'd only be in the way ... And you know how I hate all that pompiffery ..."

"Just like a man! Pleading business to get out of ..."

"It's something I have to do," implored the King. "That's right enough."

"I know," the Queen sighed. Strangely enough, she really DID know, and she understood too. But this was something she would never admit unless cornered, and so she went back to scolding. "But you've known about the Oosarians coming for weeks. Your daughter's whole future hangs in the balance. And not only that, but ..."

"Well, I doubt that," said Walterbald. In spite of himself, he grinned.

In spite of herself, and in spite of the very real worry on her mind, the Queen grinned back. And then caught herself, and frowned.

"Well, I wouldn't be too sure," she scolded. "Playing for time is all very well, but things have ways of escalating out of control, where young people are involved ..."

"It won't come to that," he argued. "And besides, you know better than anyone that binding Morainia to Oosaria will solve nothing in the long term."

"Let alone making your daughter never want to speak to you again."

"Stop," said the King. "No one will force Stormy to marry where she doesn't love. You know that."

"I know," said the Queen. "It's just that playing with people's emotions—let alone emotions as stormy as Stormy's—just ... might ... make ... things ... worse."

"You and Geraldo can handle anything the Oosarians can throw at us."

"Yes," said the Queen. "But can we handle Stormy?"

The King threw up his arms.

"AND," she went on in her grumbling voice, "it seems to me you're leaving me to do the hard stuff."

At this the King smiled again and took her hand. The Queen forced her face into a frown, but there were signs that she wasn't fooling anyone.

When he spoke next, his voice was gentle, but very, very firm. "You know me, always more a left field player than leader. I am going to the mountains because there might be something

in that cave that will help Morainia resist *them* once and for all
… for all our sakes."

He did not need to convince her. Gwynmerelda simply
did not want to him to be away so long. She looked at him in
silence, and then abruptly held open her arms. Walterbald went
to her, and they held each other.

"I'll come and kiss you goodnight."

"You'd better. Even if I'm asleep," said the Queen, letting
her face relax into a smile at last. "I'll know if you don't."

"Later," said the King, winking as he slid out of the room.

Walterbald went down the stairwell into the basement of
the castle, where he had his skolarshop. In solitude there, he
packed his specially fashioned iron digging tools, his brushes,
his notebooks. Then he smiled at a hamper of provisions left
there by the Queen.

Walterbald loved the mountains. It had been nine whole
moons since he had last been there. There was something about
their calming majesty that enabled him to think clearly. He
knew that the sort-of-cave held strange wonders, AND that the
meditative work of excavation enabled him to dig deep within
himself. He sensed there were vital clues, waiting to be found.
Clues that would guide him in addressing the threat facing
Morainia, a threat which would rear its ugly head sooner or
later.

Turning his attention to the table in front of him, he opened
an ornately carved wooden box. From the cushioning inside
it, he took out an object that was largely responsible for his
burning desire to return to the sort-of-cave.

He replayed the memory in his brain. What an expedition it had been! First he had found the mysterious egg, which being too big for him to carry back to Morainia, he had left for safekeeping with Emmeur in the mountains. Only then, at the start of the journey home, had he stumbled on the *wonderlook*.

It had been late fall and a new snow could come at any time, though the weather that day was bright blue and yellow. Walterbald had ridden over a mountain pass on a narrow, rocky, and in parts still ice-bound trail, before the descent to safer ground began. And then a glinting thing, which caught and reflected the sunlight, grabbed his eye. Probably just ice, but some inexplicable urge made him stop and take a look.

Tying his donkey to a tree, he made the awkward descent into a small valley on foot. The remaining snow was old, and where the ground peeped through it was frozen hard. The climb up the opposite south-facing slope into the sun was arduous, but not treacherous.

That was how he saw the sort-of-cave. And it was by the sort-of-cave that he found the *wonderlook*.

It was like nothing he had ever seen: an unknown shiny metal tube with a cap inset into each end. Made of a clear hard substance—not ice, not rock, not ceramic. The end pieces were, we would say, polished, and unique in the Oosarian world—unlike the opaque quality of river ice, they were completely translucent. You could see through them.

The tube was circular and almost two hands around. It was narrower at one end than the other, and extended to a little over half an arm's length. And, the most amazing thing of all, it let

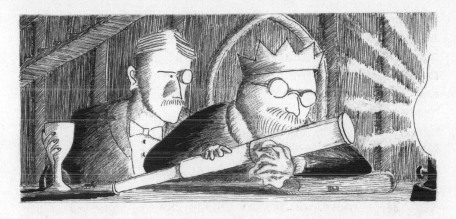

Walterbald see things never before seen. Looking through the end piece, he could see the craters of the moon, or the hairs on a deer's nostrils at a hundred paces. What we would know as a small, but powerful, telescope, Walterbald saw as a scientic marvel.

The King's mind had burned with questions, and when he brought the wonderlook back to Bald Mountain Castle, he was, with his expertise in metal-making—after a long winter of experimentation—able to master the technology of fine glass-making. First he made the spectacles that enabled Jakerbald, his father, to read the smallest words in books, which had been lost to him for many summers. Second, Walterbald made a whole array of magnifying devices which revealed the eyes of a spider, the hairs on the back of a yellow jacket, and the ability to see the world in a new and wholly amazing light.

Though he barely dared think it, for it was a blasfamy of staggering dimensions, Walterbald sensed that the sort-of-cave, and the people, or creatures, who had made the *wonderlook*, were older than any of the western peoples, perhaps even dating back to the cataclysm. Could they even have existed at the beginning time itself? He had to find out. It was as simple as that. If there were such great secrets in the past … there might be an answer to …

A knock at the door shook him from his train of thought. Geraldo entered the skolarshop, trepidation on his face. His expression changed, though, at the sight of the metal tube.

"Ah, the wonderlook," said Geraldo in awe.

"Yes. It never ceases to amaze me … Has something happened, Geraldo?"

"Aye, Walt. I've just taken a message bird." He passed the King a tightly rolled wad of paper. "It's from King Jude."

King Jude was Gwynmerelda's older brother. He had ruled Rockport, the neighboring kingdom to the south, for the past twelve summers, since their father had died.

Walterbald opened the message:

> *My spies in Oosaria reveal their ships bring strange looking men from some newly discovered island south … the strangers are somehow beholden to Oosaria, for they allow themselves to be trained, by Prince Braggardio and Prince Toromos, as soldiers in the Oosarian guard. It smells like big trouble for us … will keep you birded … J.*

Walterbald let out an audible sigh and rested his head in his hands on the table. "It is nothing less than I have been dreading," he said, and passed the note to Geraldo.

"But strange looking men from the south? What could that mean?"

"There is so much unexplored in our world, Geraldo, and it seems that the Oosarians are pushing back the frontiers of discovery in the south with their boats, as we have done a little up north. It does not really surprise me that there are other peoples. But why on earth would they want to help the Oosarians?"

"Does this affect your immediate plans any?"

The King shook his head: "I will go, but keep me informed. In an emergency, Emmeur can bring me back in a single night. You reply to Jude. Any sign that Oosaria's army is on the move and I'll be back. I just need a little time. And, I know that Morainia is as safe in your hands as it would be in mine, Geraldo."

The Vice-King smiled. "Your trust is not misplaced, Walt. Juggling the peculiarities of administration is what I love to do."

"I know it is. All power to your elbow!"

"The Order be with you, Velocidad de siete estrellas!" smiled Geraldo.

"Sevenstarspeed!" returned the King putting his fist over his own heart, and then opening his arms to hug his deputy.

Walterbald carefully wrapped the wonderlook up in its protective layers and packed it with his other things in the saddlebag. He then sat down and wrote a note to the Queen. When he was done, he sealed it with wax, blew out the candles, and headed back upstairs.

He stopped by the kitchen, fumbling around by the counter. Then he carried on up to the top floor to look in on Stormy, who was sound asleep and snoring in a most un-princessly way. Smiling, he crept down to the royal bedroom. Gwynmerelda was also sleeping. He went and sat on the edge of the bed, gazing at her. He brushed a few stray hairs from her face, gently kissing her on the lips.

"Mmmmmm, I'll miss you, too." Without opening her eyes, the Queen mumbled something about him having a safe journey and fell back into deep sleep.

Gwynmerelda had an ability, amazing to the King, to be sound asleep, but take in anything said around her, and remember it perfectly the next day as if she had been awake. If she were talking in her sleep, as she sometimes did, then Walterbald could have a conversation with her, and in the morning she would tell him how he had come into her dreams and done this or said that.

He got up from the bed. "Trust me, Gwyn. It will all work out." And though she did not reply, he felt sure she had got the message.

Chapter 3
DOES GOD GO TO THE TOILET?

When Stormy had finally fallen asleep, it was mostly dreamless at the start of the night, completely peaceful in the deep-sleep middle, but then horrifically vivid in the darkest moments before dawn end.

As happens in dreams, Stormy sort-of-knew the lay of the land. But it was all skewed. And then, as with the most vivid dreams, new realms opened up altogether.

She was in the mountains, sort-of-familiar but slightly crookedy. And then the whole foreground lurched. She let out a shriek as she fell rumble tumble … into the old world.

It was dark, not the dark of night, but a gray, cloying un-illuminated dimness, like the sun was shut out by a thundercloud of dust. It was cold, and Stormy hugged herself. She was still on the mountain, breathing heavily, and dark shapes circled above in the gloom, out of sight, but close enough for her to hear the leathery beat of their wings. As the sound receded, she could hear her own heart pounding like she had just run up the mountain trail. Somehow, some way, she knew she had to follow the trail up, up, up.

She knew she was looking for her father. Of course! He needed her help. Now she was half frantic, breaking into a run up the rocky path, her thoughts racing ahead of her, as they so often did, awake and in her dreams.

It suddenly became obvious where she was, in the way that dream logic dawns like a big bang explosion of imagination. There is nothing, and then in a sliver of a moment there is everything. Now it happened just like that.

All at once, Stormy simply knew she was inside *The Beginning Story*.

The Beginning Story, also known as *The Catastory*, is the first chapter of the wangodmatist *Book of Life*; that is, the creation myth of Morainians and of all the western peoples. In a cracked nutshell it went like this:

The Wan God created the earth in the beginning of Time, along with all the stars and planets. Many thousands of summers later when He came to visit, He exhaled from His divine lungs bringing the air and wind to earth. Rubbing His hands together, He made dirt and threw it high into the sky to be carried by the winds. Then, opening His hands skyward, fingers outstretched in a commanding god-like (what else?) gesture, He scattered seeds far and wide.

Taking a flask that hung from His hip, He spun around in a circle showering the earth with rain. As He looked on in wonder, for He never ceased to be surprised by the beauty of creation, the sun appeared from behind a cloud, making a rainbow. In one final gesture, He cupped his gigantean hands in front of His lips, blew on them, and shook them for good measure once over each shoulder, like a celestion who had just won the Milky Way Marathon. He opened His palms skyward and allowed hosts of animals to hop, skip, and fly off into their new world.

Some millions of summers later when the Wan God returned,

He was surprised to find that the animals had grown wild, and changed their shapes. They had become ravenous, and what was worse, disrespectful. When the Wan God commanded them, some sneered and snarled; some even laughed. None knew him. He knew that the bad seed had come to earth and prospered like He had never seen before.

Knowing what He must do, the Wan God brought down a punishment upon the animals of the earth. In His anger, He bellowed out loud and smashed His fists into the ground, causing volcanemons to spew forth, and earthquakes to rumble across the world. He commanded a firebolt from the stars that smashed into the earth with such force that the moon sprang from its shoulder. And with all the dust and dirt thrown into the air, a thousand-summer darkness reigned upon the earth. Speaking to the world as He departed, the Wan God said: "Know this darkness, beasts, and choke in it. But enjoy it while it lasts. For when the millennium is done, the Adaman will come and tame you and put you to work. And then you will know the wrath of the Wan God."

Heavy stuff.

In her waking life, Stormy knew all about Adaman and the Ancient Ones who the Wan God put on the earth at the end of the dark times. She had heard the story a thousand times in church, and had read it herself from *The Book of Life* in the library.

Of course not everywan believed in the Wan God. Some people, The Fool for instance, thought there was a god for every occasion.

15

Stormy did not know what she believed when she was awake. Asleep she was completely adrift, and her more playful sleeping brain was having fun retelling the beginning story.

In this version, The Wan God was doing His rounds in space and needed to stop for a bite. Taking an unusual route through the Milky Way on His way back home, He just happened upon the Earth, no more than a barren rock, really, sort-of-down-a-back-alley. He thought nothing particularly of it, and took out His packed lunch of bread and fishes. He drank water from His empyreal flask, and rested a while. Before setting off on the long journey home, He took a dump. Then, feeling refreshed and relaxed, He went on his merry way and thought nothing more about the earth. Unbeknown to the Wan God, He had picked the wrong place to do His business, for though the Wan God knew everything, He was a very busy man. His mind was on other things.

Well, after the Wan God had departed, His pee trickled away and formed the oceans. The seeds in His brown grew into plants and trees. And the worms (which the Wan God had been pretending to Himself that He did not have) crawled out of the brown and grew into the beasts.

Many thousands of summers later, in a clearing in the Great Forest, the Giggle Monkeys had fallen out, arguing over the punch line to a joke. Adamonkey had gone off in a huff. And it just so happened at this instant, by pure cosmological chance, a hefty meteorite slammed into the far side of the Earth, and then the great darkness befell the whole planet. Adamonkey found himself lost and wandering in the changed forest, until the sun shone again countless many summers later. However, during the dark times, Adamonkey had become transkinked. And while he was not the only beast to change shape, he emerged as the Adaman ... Adaman being in both of the comparative theologies, the father of men, the first of the family of Ancient Ones.

In her dream Stormy knew all this in an instant. Remember, she was battling her way up the mountain, with unseen flying-reptile creatures flapping all around in the shadows, so recreating this whole story was a neat trick. She knew she was in *The Catastory*, the dark times, which is why the Giggle Monkey view of creation sort-of made dream sense to her. She was a girl, and she was looking for her father, and she and her dad were alive *during* the dark times. Then she realized this could not be. The way the *Book of Life* told it, the first people on the earth were born *after* the dark times had ended. They were the chosen people of the Wan God put upon the earth to bring calm to the chaos. To Stormy in her dream, the thought of living through the cataclysm was more shocking than the idea of the Wan God pushing cloth.

Stormy stopped, her chest heaving. The swirling dust felt almost alive inside her, making her cough. Gasping for breath, she set off again, only able to see twenty-or-so feet ahead of her, just enough to realize that the mountain path now wound along a steep cliff. Around and around she went, spiralling up the wet and slippery path on a sort-of-fairy-tale mountain. Finally she saw the mountaintop castle above. But in that instant, the castle morphed into a gaping black cave. An ear-splitting roar came

17

from within, which seemed to shake the whole mountain.

Stormy stopped dead. She knew her father was inside.

Another roar. And then the owner of the roar emerged from the cave.

A huge black monster. A huge black cat.

It was actually an ENORMOUS black cat, with horns and electric red eyes that pierced the graydark. On two occasions in her waking life Stormy had seen the sandy colored mountain lions in the high country above Morainia. But this creature was jet black and ten times the size, so in Stormy's mind it definitely qualified as a monster. Face to face, it was even bigger than the tales mountain folk told of it in their night stories in the taverns.

"I've come to rescue my father," gasped Stormy. She was very afraid, but determined. She knew that she had to somehow get past the beast, go inside the cave, and rescue her dad. And she was going to do it, too. Just like you would for your dad. "You get out of my way," she ordered.

"Can't," rasped the beast. "Come back later. I'm busy."

"No, you're not," Stormy said. "What have you got to be busy about? If you're anything like my cat, you eat, lie around, and sleep most of the time."

"Eating sounds like a good idea," said the beast, flicking a pink tongue the width of a tree trunk across its lips.

"Now you're trying to scare me, you mean thing! What's your name, anyway?"

The Black Cat shrugged its head, and Stormy thought it looked momentarily ashamed. "Proton," he murmured. And then, regaining his momentum, he boomed, "Girlchild, know me as Proton, King of all the Mountains. Precursor of all monkeys and men."

"Oh ... 'er, I'm ... I'm Stormy," said Stormy. It seemed the right thing to say at the time. But, to Stormy's surprise, it WAS the right thing to say.

The Big Black Cat, aka Proton, King of the Mountains, Precursor of all monkeys and men, opened his electric red eyes wide.

"Ah! So it is you."

Now it was time for Stormy to open her eyes wide. "It is me what?"

"It is you who, in the stories of the Ancient Ones, brings the never ending storm to my mountains. For even though I rule here, in the absence of sunshine it seems like everyone's got a monk on all the time, and no one pays me the proper attention anymore."

Well, in that case, thought Stormy, I'll walk right on in and find my dad. She started making towards the cave in her determined way.

"What? What? What? ... What do you think you are doing?"

"Out of my way, Cat, or whatever you're called ..."

"Are you not forgetting something S-t-o-r-m-y, bringer of storms?"

"What?"

"If you wish to enter this cave, then you must bring the sunshine back to me."

Now it was Stormy's turn to stop. She was very confused.

"But I didn't bring the storm," she protested, concentrating hard. Had she brought the storm? "No! I just dreamed it and ..."

"Ah you see! You admit it." Proton laughed and began moving from foot to foot, for the entrance to the cave was not wide enough for him to pace back and forth. He looked as if he had just scored a point for the prosecution.

"No!" Stormy sobbed. "What about my dad?"

"He's busy too. Digging. But we need sunshine. Come back with some sunshine." The Cat turned to go.

"Wait!" cried Stormy.

Proton turned its head back to the girl and yawned a gaping yawn, showing stalactite and stalagmite teeth. And that curling red carpet of a tongue. "What?" he asked.

"Where do I find sunshine?"

The Cat looked mildly irritated now, like he really was being held up from having a snooze, which, as you know, all cats hate. Harrumphing, he said, "Very well! You must climb the highest mountain. And it's not this one, I've already looked. Climb the highest mountain," the Cat went on, "and you will know it at night by the constellation of the Mightor. Remember in your mind, the portion of the sky where the Mightor's arse is marked by the stars, and in the morning the sun and life will shine forth from there."

"But that's the kind of jokes that boys tell," said Stormy, trying not to laugh.

"Well I didn't make it up. Go and ask the Giggle Monkeys if you don't believe me."

In waking life, if had Stormy been able to remember these

21

fine details of this dream, she would have first thought that if Proton was King of all the mountains, then why didn't he get up off his cat ass and go and find the sunshine himself? And if she had to do it, then she would have despaired at the enormity of the task. However, in dreamtime logic it all seemed relatively straightforward and clear.

She knew the highest mountains in the world lay to the north and the east of Morainia, and the highest mountain was self-evidently one of those. All she had to do was cross hundreds of miles of unexplored wilderness, climb mountains that were previously impenetrable to humankind, and then she could map the position of the sun by the Mightor's arse, harness its energy, bring it back to Proton, and in so doing be reunited with her dad.

And just as she felt the restorative resolution of having a clear plan, the cat and the cave dissolved. The morning sun shone, and Stormy did not remember anything about her quest for sunshine.

Instead she found herself on the shore of an ocean.

On a rock, a stone's throw from the shore, sat a creature with her back to Stormy. From folk tales she knew the creature to be a Mermangel. The Mermangel seemed oblivious to Stormy, and was busy preening herself. A flutter of her wings, a swish of her tail as she combed her wet blonde locks.

And then the Mermangel stopped what she was doing and began to turn her head. For a half moment Stormy was petrified, thinking the Mermangel would have the hideous look of a devil-beast. But she had a woman's face. On closer

inspection Stormy realized that the Mermangel was her own stepmother, Gwynmerelda.

"Hello darling," said the Gwynmerangel. It seemed to Stormy like the most natural thing in the world that she would be talking to her stepmother Mermangel, in a place she had never been, while inhaling the unmistakable smell of the ocean.

"I was just coming to say goodbye," said Stormy.

"Darling child," said Gwynmerangel. "I know I cannot stop you, but I wish you would know before you go careening off all over the place, that it will most definitely end in tears."

Then Stormy woke up—just as the real sun was beginning to cast its warming rays through the gaps in the shutters of her real bedroom, making patterns of horizontal lines across the drapes. She pulled the curtains open with a swish, and the lingering fragments of her mad dreams disappeared.

Chapter 4
THE WILSONS AND THE GODLOVES

Wance upon a time there was a beautiful princess, named
Alexandra Stormybald Wilson. Stormy lived in a sort-of-
castle on Bald Mountain, with her father the King Walterbald
Wilson the Second, and her sort-of-ugly, sort of-but-maybe-not-
evil stepmother, Queen Gwynmerelda. Bald Mountain Castle
was in the territory of Morainia, which was a small and fairly
isolated part of a much larger and much unexplored world.

Had Walterbald been writing the story, he would have begun
it with the words *Wance upon a World*, for Time, as you and
I know it, had not yet been invented in Morainia. And if we
begin to dig, as we shall inevitably have to do as we accompany
a thirteen-year-old princess suddenly let loose, then we shall
discover that there was something about this world that was not
at all right. King Walterbald knew something of this, and that
was why he was going on his expedition: to find out more.

For Walterbald, in his quest for knowledge, had become
aware in recent summers that there were certain ideas people
knew and took for granted, which had always seemed to fit
with the lore of this fairy tale world, but which increasingly, to
a logically enquiring mind like his own, were all out of whack.

The house on Bald Mountain was a sort-of-castle, because
while it was certainly spacious by contemporary standards (it
had to accommodate various members of the King and Queen's

extended families, and had to have a barn attached that was big enough for large gatherings of more than fifty people), this castle was made almost entirely of wood. And to the honest eye, it could reasonably be described as ramshackle. There were metal fixings, but these were always used wisely and sparingly, because workable metal was a rare commodity, even in Morainia. Although there were rumors ...

Notable among the castle's other inhabitants were the widowed Grandma Natasha Godlove, the Queen Mother. Grandma Godlove, or Gigi as she was affectionately known, and her granddaughter Stormy got on like a house on fire. Then there was Grandma Zilpher and Grandpa Jakerbald Wilson, the King's parents.

These were a handful to say the least—cantankerous and contrary with each other, and more so with their own children. And if it does not seem to make sense that Jakerbald Wilson was alive and yet Walterbald was King, fretter ye not.

We all know about Queen Mothers, but the idea of a King Father seems strange. But why should it be—ask yourself that. And anyway, Jakerbald was only strange when he played Grandpa-ish tricks. He was actually a very cheery and highly intelligent fellow. Highly original in his outlook, although, it must be admitted, a bit ornery.

It was in keeping with his ornery character that when Jakerbald reached his fifty-fifth birthday, he took the unusual step of retiring, becoming the first known King Father, and causing a proper constitutional storm in a water tank.

Most people in Morainia were wangodmatists to some

degree or other, at least on the surface. But most were too busy with daily life to be more involved than attending Seventh day services and religious festivals. Wangodmatism had its professional holy men, called probbers, missioned throughout the western lands. And the ruling body of wangodmatists in Morainia, the unimaginatively named High Council of Wangodmatists, had seen Jakerbald's resignation as an in.

The probbers said that the whole Wilson family should thus be excluded from the throne. They'd never liked those Wilsons anyway—all of them too lively by half. And the Council suspected they were a bunch of Freethinkers to boot. That Jakerbald! And Walterbald was worse! And no male heir! Of course they saw an opportunity to make their own man, Probber Rogerley Bishop, the new King. Or at least someone with a couple of sons.

The more pragmatic Council of Town Elders said it really should go to a vote, because even if it WAS a kingdom, the Council of Town Elders knew you only could lead when you led where people wanted to go. So four prospective kingdidates were put forward, including Bishop and Walterbald. In the event, when it was put to a popular vote, despite the dirty-trickery and shenanigans of the wangodmatists, the Morainian people decided that Walterbald should be King after all. And not purely out of a respect for tradition. They liked Walterbald. That was the long and short of it. And he was useful, King or no.

As a young man, Walterbald had pioneered the development of the first septic tanks in the town, which had improved the humor and health of all. And then he had invented a wind-powered water pump. The prototype lifted water a distance of three hundred vertical feet, from the irrigation ditch right into a water tank in the basement of Bald Mountain Castle. This technology had the wider and very popular application of making the watering of naturally drier benches above the ditch a hundred times easier. And in extending the Morainian commonlands, suddenly Morainians had the capacity to engage in proper crop rotation, averting the risk of over-farming some of the available land. In short, agricultural output achieved a stable level, which made (almost) everyone happy therein, for even in sort-of-fairy tale worlds, everyone has to eat.

Walterbald was always tinkering with things, trying to make them work better. Just like what he was doing now, in going north to the mountains. Trying to make his world work better. But enough of politics and pumpery ... for hark, fellow travelers, the cock crows forth already. And there are many early risers in Bald Mountain Castle.

Chapter 5
GOOD NEWS BAD NEWS

Queen Gwynmerelda was already up and doing yoga. She was a striking figure, even when stood on her head, which allowed the blood from her feet to refresh her brain and temporarily squish her face. Righting herself, and passing from the bedroom to the bathroom, Gwynmerelda was neither as ugly nor as evil as *our* traditions might have led us to believe. Not even when she sat on the toilet. For if the jury was still out on whether the Wangod had bodily functions, the queens in this world, unlike those in our own, most certainly did go to the toilet.

Naturally, the King did not find her to be either ugly or evil, or any such trad stepmother things. While beauty is in the eye of the beholder, and evil doings can rapidly diminish first impressions of beauty, Queen Gwynmerelda (at forty summers) still held the King enthralled. Furthermore, she was a practical, active woman, and these are very good traits for a wife as well as a queen. Gwynmerelda could be self-centered and insensitive at times, but these are hardly unusual attributes among humans. And if she lacked tact, beneath it all she did have a heart.

Of course Stormy was a teenage Princess who had lost her own mother, Queen Ursula, on the night of her birth. And things being what they were, it wasn't likely that the stormy

Princess and her stepmother would get along. And they didn't. But even Stormy had to admit, at least to herself in secret, that Gwynmerelda ran a tight ship in Bald Mountain Castle.

For example, Gwynmerelda believed in everyone pulling her or his own weight. While traditional kings and queens had serving people to satisfy their every whim and fancy, at Bald Mountain Castle the Wilson family fended for itself. The Queen made sure Stormy was well versed in washing up, and was quite able to make her own omelettes, bake bread, roll her own pasta, and shoot, skin, and cook a rabbit.

"It'll come in handy," Gwynmerelda would say sternly when Stormy groaned, "Do I HAVE to?" "You'll see." And if a Queen can say that to a Princess, it's probably true.

While the Wilsons sometimes did have helpers from the town to cook and clean, this was in return for hands-on services provided by members of the royal household themselves.

Gwynmerelda taught yoga and ran a women's group. Walterbald was called on for advice on any number of things. If anything mechanical needed fixing, he rolled up his sleeves and got dirt under his fingernails.

There was a tradition of service in Stormy's country. All Morainians over the age of twelve, for example, trained with the Morainian Defense Guard. And for such a small and isolated kingdom, the home guard had seen active service down through its history more than you might think. The previous summer, Stormy had trained with the Cliff Scouts. The Cliff Scouts patrolled hidden trails in the steep forest above the Bald River, from where they could monitor the Falls Road without being seen. Stormy had particularly enjoyed the training runs from base to summit of the Falls Road, which suited her natural talents.

Stormy also volunteered at the library. There were reading books there, but it was mostly picture books, because most people could not read. Stormy, who could read quite well (trust Gwynmerelda for that!), sometimes read aloud to children and adults. Each book was hand-crafted, and hand-written or drawn, as the printing press, let alone the computers—which most children in our time use the library for—had not been imagined. No eating sweets while reading or dog-earing the pages here!

Today, in fact, was her day to volunteer. And because she had chores to do, Stormy was up, as usual, as early as the Queen.

Sonia the summer kitchen girl had already helped pack the King off on his travels, so when Stormy got to the kitchen, there was food on the table. Stormy knew Sonia's cousin Fred, one of the senior Cliff Scouts. They chatted about him as the Princess tore off hunks of still-warm bread, smothering them with gooseberry jam. There was rough cereal and goat-milk, too, along with goat-cheese and a wooden bowl brimful with some of the first fresh strawberries of the season. There was tea in the pot, not tea as you or I might know it, but locally gathered and dried leaves infused in boiling water. It was actually as good a feast as you could hope for, and Stormy tucked in with full teen gusto.

"Our Fred says you're not bad on them runs, for a princess, anyways," Sonia teased Stormy. "I think he's got a crush on you."

Stormy blushed, but didn't answer.

The grandparents filed in one after another and began piling up their plates while mumbling among themselves. Last but not least came Gwynmerelda. She entered the room radiating a yogatic splendor that deserved a fanfare, as was usual with her. But it never ceased to seriously irritate her stepdaughter.

Seating herself regally and taking a cup of tea, Gwynmerelda composed herself. But someone paying close attention would have noticed that composure was hard won. Gwynmerelda was worried. But she was a Queen, and queens, she felt, dealt with their worries on their own. This may have been why she dealt with this particularly worry with less finesse than she might have.

"Now Alexandra," she began in a too-stepmotherly voice. "As I am sure your father told you last night, we have special guests, very special guests arriving this afternoon."

It was something in the Queen's tone. Stormy stopped chewing.

"But I'm volunteering at the library."

"Oh don't worry about that. I've already told Athiane you won't be going in today." The Queen sighed to herself. She knew she was handling this badly, but not knowing another way, forged ahead.

"Hmmm," she said more sternly than she felt, "I sense your father has left me again to be the bearer of important tidings. Well ..." And then she rushed through the very news that worried her: "This afternoon Prince Mercurio will arrive, accompanied by Queen Nukeander, from, as you all know, our neighbors, the kingdom of Oosaria."

Grandpa Jakerbald spat out a mouthful of tea in surprise. Grandma Zilpher and Gigi looked very uncomfortable.

"But they don't like us!" Stormy said. "The last time they were here, Mercurio said we all smiled too much. And they're such a downer. Why are they coming here?"

There was silence in the room. It was well known in Morainia that if there was an invasion of that peaceful country, it would be from Oosaria. So the grandparents had a good idea what was coming next.

"Grandma? Grandpa?" Stormy said. But no one answered her.

The Queen, determined, carried on. "They come, I believe, to make a proposal that will join our two kingdoms in peace."

Stormy laughed. "Oh yeah," she said. "Fred always says if anyone's going to invade us, it'll be ..."

"They come to make a MARRIAGE proposal." The Queen sipped her tea with apparent calm. "This is a courtship visit. And an official one, too."

At this, Stormy was stunned into silence. Not for long, however. As the news sunk in, her face reddened and her eyes flashed.

"No way. No way am I ever marrying that toadying prancer. I won't even be NICE to him."

"And who, may I ask, told you that you would have any choice in the matter?" snapped the Queen. She hated herself for sounding like this, but a combination of worry, guilt, and annoyance at her teenage stepdaughter now had control.

"I'd rather die," said Stormy, and she burst into tears. All three grandparents jumped up at once, clucking sympathetically around her. And then there was a different sound, like someone banging a hammer on the church gong.

It was The Fool, bedraggled and spindly as usual, three-cornered hat askew and looking somewhat hung over, announcing his entrance by banging a metal serving spoon on an upheld frying pan.

"Oh bugger, late as usual," he muttered. And then, gathering himself together, The Fool did his Fool thing:

> *The finery, the pomp, the regaliocol,*
> *The marriage-brokery all arranged.*
> *But if the best-laid plans were unstoppable ...*
> *Then there would be no story strange ...*

The Fool was curious in the sense that he was not especially good at his craft. He could make astute observations in the form of rhyme, but was not particularly funny. In the way of failed performers everywhere, he would have made a good teacher in the craft of Fooldom. Or maybe it was all a clever disguise?

Meanwhile, Queen Gwynmerelda felt she'd had just about enough. Why was it always only her who worried about the future of the kingdom? The rest of them just enjoyed themselves. "Shut the feckle up," she snapped.

Everyone turned and looked inquiringly her way.

"Nukeander's retinue is on its way, and the Princess will not only meet the Prince, but she will be on her very best behavior," said the Queen, eyeing Stormy with a particularly stern look.

"No, I won't! I can't stand that brat of a buttstart."

"Well," said The Fool, searching for the right words. "Well, you will have to meet him, Stormy ... but only because it will take us a few days or so to get ready."

"Get ready for what?" demanded the Queen.

"Why, to depart of course."

At this, Stormy saw the faintest glimmer of light at the end of what was looking like some very dark days indeed. She looked hopefully at The Fool, and so didn't notice a certain relaxing of a worried line on the Queen's forehead. The Fool did his Fool Thing again:

> *The east wind blows a change in atmosphere*
> *That reacts ill in our western heavens*
> *Never did it ever look so black here*
> *Since the dark age of the cataclysm*

And defying his always-about-to-fall-over appearance, The Fool stood on Walterbald's empty chair at the head of the table and pronounced: "Let all present bear witness. I hereby initiate Princess Stormy into the Order of the Accidental Adventurers!"

He looked at Stormy, and Stormy found herself nodding vigorously, without knowing what she was agreeing to. Plucking it from nowhere, The Fool threw an oversized egg at the Princess, which splattered across the top of her left ear.

"Ow! What was that for?" howled Stormy.

Nobody answered.

The grandparents began a low murmuring. Sonia the kitchen girl, who had been hovering with a fresh round of bread, dropped the wooden bowl, and was scurrying down on her hands and knees to clear up the mess. The Queen, unseen by the rest, exchanged a quick look with The Fool. She then rose to her feet, the scraping back of her huge chair demanding silence.

"You call that an initiation, you idiot?"

"Skimble-skamble it is not. Princess Alexandra," said The Fool, looking at Stormy and winking, "The Princess, is, if I am not mistaken, thirteen summers old. And thus in accordance with ancient regaliocol, as I am sure you, dear Queen, are more aware than most, those who have been initiated into the Order are bound to embark upon the journey in search of Accidental Adventure."

"She's a girl, you dunderheaded moonkid," the Queen said. At this, Gigi looked at her queerly. Ah, the old woman thought to herself. She's my daughter, and I know she's up to something.

"But she's heir to the throne," The Fool retorted. "That is, if we don't persist with the elective monarchy anomaly." And with that, the whole breakfast table was thrown into constitutional crisis.

Jakerbald stood up, a smile spreading across his face, and began to clap his hands, saying "Bravo! Bravo!" Having once been King and a member of the Order himself, he raised his mug of apple juice to propose: "A toast to Princess Alexandra Stormybald Wilson ... groundbreaking ... a better granddaughter one couldn't hope to have ... Welcome to the Order of the—"

"Sit down you wizened gracklebrain," said the Queen, cutting him off. And in that moment, the only King of Morainia in the last seventy-five summers to have led men into battle (defensive though it was) quaked in the shadow of his daughter-in-law.

In the pregnant pause, The Fool deftly leapt on to the table, then skipped along its whole length, bearing down on the Queen. Gwynmerelda lunged at him, as The Fool jumped past her in an impossible bound towards the counter at the far end of the kitchen—his arms outstretched to reach the biscuit tin on the toppermost shelf.

Gwynmerelda had slowed The Fool's momentum, but his reaching fingers still managed to send the tin clattering across the floor, while The Fool himself landed in a heap.

On impact, the tin sent its contents flying, with biscuit crumbs and a sealed notandum skittering across the floor. The note was sealed with the King's waxen emblem—a crown guarded by a ravenbird on either side.

At a look from the Queen, Sonia bent down, picked up the note, and handed it to Gwynmerelda, who was now seated, calm and queenly, at the head of the table. The Queen wielded her bread knife, sliced open the wax, and unfolded the paper. All eyes upon her saw her brief look of resignation as she read the words contained within. Gwynmerelda sighed.

"Well what does it say?" piped up Jakerbald.

"Let her read it," said Grandma Zilpher.

Gigi, who sat next to Stormy, put a protective arm around the Princess's shoulder, as if fearing bad tidings. Stormy herself was reeling, her emotions pulled this way then that. It felt like her life had changed forever in the short space of time between last night and now.

"It says," said the Queen, "that Princess Alexandra is to be accompanied by The Fool, on a totally fruitless journey, seeking a ridiculous Accidental Adventure, which everyone knows has traditionally been used by Morainian men as an excuse to get off by themselves."

"You're embellishing," said The Fool, grinning. "What else?"

"Whatever else it says, it does not concern you."

On the contrary, what the note said did concern The Fool, and everyone else around the table. A cloud passed in front of the sun in the sky outside, and the shadow that passed through the kitchen, over the Queen's face, masked something in her expression. It went unnoticed by all except for Gigi, the Queen's own mother. Then, quick as a splash, Gwynmerelda's regal demeanor returned.

Queen Gwynmerelda stood up, sending her chair clunking over, and puffing herself up, she looked directly into Stormy's eyes.

"Princess Alexandra. Queen Nukeander and the royal Prince Mercurio will be arriving by midday, and you better be on your very best behavior my girl, or woe betide the consequences."

In the pandemonium that followed, almost no one noticed the note fall to the floor, where Sonia, the kitchen maid, swept it up before leaving the room. Only Stormy saw. But she had other things to think about just then.

Chapter 6
BIG HAIR, BIG TROUBLE

Remember, that Time as we know it had not been invented in the western kingdoms. Morainians did not yet think in terms of minutes and hours. They had long days and short days according to the season; they had their arbitrary seven-day week, and worked in lunar months and solar years. But anything shorter was measured in moments. Yes, they had their moments, but these were fluid, and of variable and thus indeterminate length.

As you may have guessed, the clock, which Morainians had never encountered, was ticking towards the hour when they would. But for Stormy, the morning and afternoon were a jumble of emotions that went on forever. While she wanted the meeting with the Prince Mercurio to be over and done with, she also wished it could be put off for as long as possible.

Queen Nukeander, her second youngest son Prince Mercurio, a Godmatist probber named Elijareen, and their entourage of journey-men and maids, arrived mid-afternoon.

There was a crazy commotion as their convoy wound its way through the narrow streets of Morainia town. Donkey-drawn carriages were highly unusual in these parts, and the ornate extravagance of workmanship on Queen Nukeander's carriage was rarely seen by the mountain townfolk. Gold-painted wooden swirls swelled above the front wheels into cascading waves. Over each of the rear wheels sat a finely carved seraphic Mermangel, complete with wings, curling fishtails, and swirling golden hair, which cascaded around their beguiling blue ocean eyes and red sunset lips. Arms outstretched along either side of the carriage windows, the Mermangels dwarfed the peering face of Prince Mercurio.

The whole charabanc spoke of untold wealth in the sea kingdoms to the south.

Stormy heard the fanfare as the procession wound its way up Bald Mountain and through the front gate. She saw the royal carriage lurch a bit on account of a pothole in the driveway. And while imagining the Mermangel's head torn off by a collision with the wall, Stormy experienced a momentary wisp of that morning's forgotten dream. But then the dream was gone, and she watched the visitors disembark, to be greeted by Geraldo.

A sudden shooting pain in her stomach made Stormy cramp-up double. And though she had recovered when Gigi arrived to help her dress for dinner, the combination of the strange pain and the disturbing circumstance, made her feel weak and sad. So even though she had never gone in for big frocks and big hair, this time she didn't put up her usual protest. She needed all her concentration to face the challenge of whatever the night's protocol and pompiffery would throw at her.

When Gigi ushered Stormy into Gwynmerelda's chamber for a queenly seal of approval, Stormy caught a hurried and secretive exchange between the daughter and mother. This made Stormy feel even less at ease, if that was possible. But it was a fleeting impression, and Gwynmerelda was immediately back to her old self, primping a stray hair among the elegantly styled curls bunched up on Stormy's head.

"I have always told you, Alex, that you scrub up particularly well, given the right guidance." And then with a burst of warmth, which again seemed strange for Gwynmerelda, she said. "You will be absolutely fine, my dear. Absolutely fine." Straightening her back in that regal, yoga-trained way she had, the Queen indicated that the Princess do the same. Taking Stormy's hand, she led her to meet the Handsome Prince.

Maybe it was true. As the stories told, the charming Prince would come, and he would be handsome beyond belief. He would sweep the Princess off her feet, and this would be the start of their living happily ever after ...

In spite of her earlier words, Princess Stormy found herself gazing to her right, along the dinner table toward Prince Mercurio. Had she been able to admit it to herself, her heart cogs were almost imperceptibly beginning to engage. It was like a butterfly emerging from a chrysalis inside her stomach, and beating its wings for the very first time.

Mercurio was older than Stormy, of course. He was nineteen. He was tall, blonde, handsome; he looked mature. Stormy had met him before, but then she had only been six summers old, and he twelve. There had been a big celebration feast when Walterbald married Gwynmerelda, and it would have been a mistake not to invite representatives of the kingdom of Oosaria. The young Prince had come with his mother, Nukeander, the

Queen and ruler of Oosaria. And all Stormy could remember of Mercurio was hating him for how he teased her, by pulling the limbs from a daddy long-legs. She vaguely remembered that he'd said there should be war, not feasting, between their peoples. And that a good battle would settle once and for all who owned what. But maybe her memory was playing tricks on her?

All that was all a long time ago. And in the interim, Mercurio had seemingly changed into a man, as Stormy knew that she herself was beginning to change from a girl to a young woman.

All this arranged marriage business may seem strange to us, but in this sort-of-fairy-tale world, people generally died young. Stormy's mother Ursula, for instance. It was highly unusual for someone of Stormy's age to have three living grandparents. Jakerbald, at the age of sixty-six, was as old and wise a man as you would usually ever meet.

And so it followed that if children were to have grandparents, and grandparents were to know their grandchildren, then it was not out of the ordinary for teenage girls to give birth to children, fathered by swashbuckling teenage boys, in arranged teenage marriages.

Stormy leaned forward again and looked over to the swaggerswanking Mercurio, before lowering her eyes to the plate where she'd mostly just pushed the food around. It didn't matter that the braised wild turkey and fire-roasted potatoes were her favorite.

The Prince seemed most charming, in a way that Stormy

could not explain. He could talk at the dinner table like an adult. According to tradition, Mercurio sat to the right of Queen Gwynmerelda. Nukeander sat to Gwynmerelda's left, and Stormy to Nukeander's left. This meant that for Mercurio and Stormy to see each other, one or both of them had to lean conspicuously forwards to look around the two queens. Of course this was the whole point. In this way, everyone else around the table, and the two queens in particular, would be acutely aware of any electrical currents. It was an age-old ritual, which had probably evolved specifically to play havoc with teenage hormones.

Stormy watched her stepmother smiling and laughing at Mercurio's small talk. She felt very uncomfortable. Her brain told her one thing and her body another; she could not decide which one of them was lying to her. Between the struggle of body and brain, she was having a hard time keeping up her end of the conversation. She managed to *mmm* and *aaa*, and grunt at Nukeander's attempts to engage her, but little else.

Some short moons back, Stormy had had a crush on a boy who was staying in town. Indeed, they had on one occasion secretly kissed. It was sweet and fleeting, for the boy, named River, was with a band of travelling players performing in Morainia for the Spring Fayre. It seemed like he'd gone away as soon as he had appeared.

Then there was Fred, from the Cliff Scouts. Stormy liked Fred, but not like she had liked River. But Fred seemed to like Stormy the way she'd liked River. It was all very confusing.

Stormy felt some more of these exciting uncertainties as she furtively leaned forward and glanced at Mercurio again. This time he caught her eye and she quickly looked away. Nukeander caught the moment, as did Gwynmerelda; they turned to each other and exchanged knowing looks.

Unusually, Stormy had been allowed a glass of the reddest wine she had ever seen. And where she had trouble making the food pass her lips, she had no problem with the wine. Each time she drank, the glass was magically refilled, the wine imperceptibly cloudier, and Stormy drank some more.

Then the dinner was suddenly over. The band struck up, and the dancing began, led by Zilpher and Jakerbald, who only needed the slightest excuse to take to the dance floor. Most of the adults gradually followed suit. Stormy saw all this as a pleasant blur, and then Mercurio took her hand and led her to the dance floor. She felt like she was walking on air.

Stormy's head was spinning from too much wine with too little food. And the movement as she and Mercurio circulated the dance floor did nothing to help her regain any sense of balance. She felt dizzy and thrilled at the same time. She wondered if this was what people meant when they described being swept off their feet by a special other.

But when she dared raise her head and look into Mercurio's blue eyes, what she saw unnerved her—and not in a good way. That uncomfortable moment, however, was quickly snatched away. For just as suddenly as it had begun, the dance was over, and everyone was applauding. Indeed, everyone had made a half circle around the Prince and Princess and were cheering them. Mercurio whispered something in Stormy's ear, but

she couldn't hear what he said. She just felt his hot wet breath against her ear. She didn't like it, and turned to walk away.

Soon the evening's guests began melting away, as people wished each other good night. Stormy felt Mercurio squeeze her hand as he drifted away. She felt Gwynmerelda hugging her, and Zilpher and Gigi taking hold of her hands. The combination of emotions and events made the weather systems in Stormy's stomach billow in unpredictable formations.

The way Stormy remembered it, Mercurio was staring up at her with an uncomfortable glint in his eye, as she somehow managed to climb the stairwell. She saw Nukeander go to him, take him by the arm, and say something angrily. He shook his mother's arm off and came up the stairs after her. The next thing she knew, she was in the corridor just before her own bedroom. But Mercurio was now in front of her, leaning against the doorjamb of her room. His eyes still had that same glint. And something about that glint made Stormy afraid.

Chapter 7
ONE DEAD PRINCE

She must be dreaming she thought. She closed her eyes and shook her head. A dizziness swirled up from her stomach, and when she opened her eyes again, Mercurio was still there, coming towards her.

Mercurio grabbed Stormy by the wrists and pushed her against the door. Before she had time to breath he was kissing her, pushing his tongue against her mouth.

As she struggled, Stormy's elbow caught the door handle, pressing down upon it, releasing the door inwards, and sending the Prince and Princess sprawling. Freed from Mercurio's gropple, Stormy leapt onto the bed. "What are you DOING?" she cried, as Mercurio closed the door behind him and bolted it.

"Stay away from me," she screamed.

"Fear me not, little strumpet," grinned Mercurio. "I only want a quiet word."

And she half believed him—for the half-moment it took until he lunged at her legs, sending her spinning backwards into the pillows. Immediately he was on her again, holding down her arms. His eyes bore down into Stormy's, but his voice was amused, almost casual, when he said, "You will marry me." And then he said, "Almost I think it will be a pleasure to break you." He grinned again. "I always loved a fight."

Stormy looked into his cold blue eyes and saw the truth

there: no love, but hatred. And she learned one of the first lessons of her adult life—that there are those who prefer the one to the other. It was a hard lesson, and she had no time to take it in, as he pulled her up toward him.

She gave a small sob, and realized her mistake. But her distress only added more fuel to Mercurio's fire.

Mercurio really did want to marry Stormy. It was his ticket to being the next King of Morainia. Having two older brothers before him, and vying to be next in line to the Oosarian throne, this was his one big chance. He wasn't going to miss out. Drunk as he was, he thought there was no time like the present to assert his authority. Mercurio, it will be seen, had never been able to wait for what he wanted.

He laughed again and repeated. "You will marry me. My interests will be yours. What's yours will be mine. And that includes your precious Morainian metals, deep in these hills." He closed his eyes as if savoring her dowry already.

That was a mistake.

In that instant Stormy managed to wriggle partially free. Unseating the Prince, she forced her knees up in front of her, and with the tautness of a crossbow, kicked out with all her might. Her heels crunched into Mercurio's ribs. He let out a surprised groan, and fell backwards.

Stormy curled up in a defensive ball, burying her head in the bed, expecting the worst. Bracing herself for the inevitable onslaught ...

... A nonillionth of a moment become a nano-moment, that stretched and split. Those two nano-moments then elasticated and split again, like cells dividing and replicating. Four became eight; eight became sixteen, and so on exponentially … The attack never came. There was only silence.

Slowly, very slowly, Stormy lifted her head and turned. Through her tears she looked and saw the Prince sprawled on the wooden floor, looking up with a fixed expression on his face, and a pool of blood spreading from the back of his head. She saw blood on the bedpost. Then there was a banging on the door and shouting.

Mechanically, Stormy lifted her legs over the side of the bed and began to walk, stepping around the dead prince, to the door. She slid the bolt back, opened the door, and stood aside as Gwynmerelda rushed in. Geraldo came behind her, quickly shutting the door behind him.

Chapter 8
YOGA BREATH

Stormy threw herself at Gwynmerelda, burying her head in the queen's breast, as if by shutting her eyes tightly, she could make it all go away.

The Queen took in the grisly scene with one look. "I knew it," she said grimly. "That look on his face ..."

Geraldo bent over the Prince—or, more accurately, what had been the Prince—and said dispassionately, "Little bastard. He must have cracked his skull when you fought him off."

Stormy nodded mutely.

"My fault," said Gwynmerelda tensely. "We used you to gain time. But there's no time now. We have to get you away from here."

"Can I sleep ... can I come to your room?" the Princess whimpered.

"No— I mean, yes, come to my room, but we have to get you away ... away from the castle ... tonight."

"I'm afraid so, Stormy," nodded Geraldo, as a look of bewildered horror crept across the Princess's already confuzzled brow. "There is no seer living who could predict what the Oosarians might do now. We have to get you as far away and as fast as possible. For your own safety," he continued, putting a finger to his lips and ushering them out of the room. Geraldo closed the door on the dead Prince.

"Take Stormy downstairs," he said, looking at Gwynmerelda.

"Yes," she whispered back. "You wake The Fool."

The Queen led Stormy quietly down the back staircase and into her own chamber, where she briskly checked through a knapsack she had hidden, already packed. Stormy watched, barely understanding what this meant. Had the Queen known the Oosarian visit would have unintended consequences?

What Gwynmerelda really wanted to do was to fold the frightened Princess in her arms and reassure her. But for her own safety, Stormy would have to be able to stand on her own now. She had to learn she was alone. "Don't stand there looking like a goggle bird, Girl," she barked. "Move!"

The harshness had its intended effect. Stormy angrily came out of her trance and set to work.

"Packing for a camping trip, ladies?" The Fool stuck his head in the door. He had been pleasantly drunk and fast asleep, but the news that he must shortly leave sobered him up quick.

Tearful goodbyes were out of the question. Gwynmerelda knew that any sign of sentiment now would only hamper Stormy. So with dry eyes and unyielding body, the Queen pushed Stormy and The Fool out into the night.

She watched as they disappeared, hurrying, into the dark, and didn't blink once, not even when Stormy looked back uncertainly one last time. It was only when the Queen knew they were gone that she allowed herself a brief moment of collapse. She sank back against the wall, gasping for air.

Geraldo looked at her, worried. "Yoga breath!" he advised.

"Yes. Yes," she said. And the deep breaths did indeed help restore her regal balance. Because for a Queen—and for all of us—sometimes duty comes first. And duty is hard. It is hard to send a child out into the world to become an adult. But it has to be done.

"We'll wait until dawn," she said tensely. "Before we rouse the Oosarians. We have to give Stormy and The Fool what little head start we can."

Geraldo nodded.

Yoga breath again. And a silent prayer—that no one would hear the muted patter of the donkeys carrying The Fool and Stormy from the rear stable, to a mountain trail, and into the night.

No one in the castle stirred. And there was no sound until just before dawn—the screams of Queen Nukeander, who had woken early and gone in search of her son. She, who knew her son well, had known in which bedroom to first look.

Gwynmerelda looked grimly at Geraldo and said, "I'll go to her. And you …"

He nodded. He knew what he had to do.

In a side chamber, Rogerley Bishop, the highest-ranking Morainian probber, was discussing matters with Elijareen, the Oosarian probber.

"You planned this?" Elijareen asked coolly.

"No, no, no," replied Bishop with a satisfied smile. "Would that I had any influence over that reckless girl. But it does rather, shall we say, change things?"

"Meaning?"

"Meaning people understand a war of revenge."

As indeed they do, in every world. And this sort-of world was no different from any other in needing a seen-to-be-respectable reason for warring against a neighbor.

This, Stormy had now provided. One dead Prince was a good reason. Even if it was an accident.

56

Chapter 9
A GIG AT THE GRACKLE TAVERN

S tormy and The Fool rode their donkeys relentlessly north and west. It was a mostly cloudy, moonless night, and not at all easy going on the less well-used trails. Only the occasional glimpse of the pole star gave them reassurance.

By midmorning they were heading high into the mountains. The sun rose and warmed their backs. It felt like Spring. As the trail wound its way skyward towards an unseen pass, particular zigs or zags gave them brief glimpses of a snow-covered peak, beyond which lay the Great Ice Wall.

They rode on, not daring to stop for rest, reached the mountain pass by late afternoon, and began their descent into the next valley over. The sun cast its glare on a lake far below. It would be nightfall soon.

"We need to go into a town," The Fool said, worried. "There is a place I know down below. We can rest there."

As the warm day melted into twilight, The Fool and the Princess entered the small lakeside town of Wangodmanchia. There were few people on Main Street, but Stormy didn't dare raise her head to look at their faces. Her attention, anyway, was drawn to a low noise coming from a leaning building down at the end of the street. As they neared, the noise of boisterous voices got louder, and Stormy could see the decrepit look of the building, which was wholly out of place among the austere and well-kept houses of the town.

"Here it is," said The Fool, thinking to himself it had been a long time. "The gobstained Grackle Tavern." Dismounting and indicating Stormy do the same, he whispered, "Trust me!" He helped her down and hitched the donkeys to the rail. "It'll just be one drink, and you'll be in a comfy bed before you know it. We just have to establish our presence, so people won't think anything of it. Follow my lead and you'll be fine."

Pushing open the doors, they entered the Tavern. The noise and smells hit Stormy full in the face. It was busy inside, and nobody in particular looked at them as they found a small table away from the bar.

If you HAD looked at The Fool and Stormy, you would not think them to be an entertainer and a Princess. You would think them an entertainer, and, well, another (possibly apprentice) entertainer.

This is exactly what the first person to notice Stormy thought, anyway.

"Oooh, why the long face, Miss? Life's too short," said the brash young Tavernmizz.

Stormy looked at The Fool. The Tavernmizz looked from Stormy to The Fool and asked in a friendly voice, "What will it be then? Some fresh ale to enliven your thezzpian livers? And then you'll play us some romp-pomp-pum-paggle, I shouldn't wonder."

The Fool nodded.

"What," said Stormy below her breath to The Fool, "is she talking about?

"She thinks," said The Fool, smiling his first natural smile of the day, "that we are travelling players."

Before Stormy could reply, the Tavernmizz had plumped two jars of ale on the table before them. And in spite of the wine-wracked traumas of the night before, Stormy took the jug by the horns with a great gulp of the beer.

"That's better innit?" laughed the Tavernmizz. "You are sixteen?" she went on, taking a stern, closer look at Stormy. "Only jokin'. I knows you are, luvvy." Then, as some other reveler loudly called her attention, the Tavernmizz wheeled away

The Fool broke the spell first and looked at the now slightly less bedraggled Stormy. "Tastes good eh?" he said as Stormy took another gulp.

She nodded. She hadn't realized how thirsty she was, or how hungry.

"We'll get food," he reassured her, as if reading her thoughts.

As The Fool was looking around for signs of what food might be on offer, and trying to attract the attention of the Tavernmizz again, there was a ruckus behind them at the front door. Three soldiers were blustering their way in.

Suddenly The Fool was alert, fox-like animal radar attuned.

"Change of plan," he said under his breath to Stormy. "My girl! The Great God Joke could not have thought us up a better disguise."

Stormy looked at him flummoxed.

"What do you mean?"

"Just follow my lead! I know you can do it."

And with the words *do what?* frozen on Stormy's lips, The Fool stood up with gravitas that only draped his spindly form when he engaged in the plying of his trade.

> *Fellow swillers, sit back, relax, hush-be-still,*
> *I have news, I command your attention.*
> *Take a slug, let the ale tickle your tonsils,*
> *And hold your belief in suspension.*
>
> *We tell a tale of many terrors and a girl caught between,*
> *A rock and a life on the run.*
> *On the wrong side of a vengeful warrior queen*
> *Who held the girl murdered her son.*

The crowd cooed. And then The Fool looked to Stormy, with a slight nod of his head, as a musician would to his band mates, indicating that she come in with her part.

Not quite comprehending, Stormy felt her legs act on their own, bringing her to standing, and the muscles in her face contorting, shaping a begoggled "oh" shape, as if about to launch into song.

A murmur to her right, and she saw the soldiers and instantly understood. Her discomfort fell away like a loosely tied cloak. She lifted her arms in an opening theatrical gesture and half sang:

I killed him! That is I mean I kissed him. That is the girl,
In this tale did long ago.
He didn't deserve that, but he was drunk beyond lewd.
I shoved him off, and his head cracked a post.

"To die ... eugh ... at the hands of an undergirl,"
The Prince cried as he gasped his last breath.
"I was meant for great things, you are cursed now you ...
girl,
And my mother will hunt you to death."

Boys! Always the same. When things go wrong,
They go crying to mom.
And this one would never have made a good king,
Carrying on like he did with his ... thing.

At this Stormy paused, for the whole place was in uproar,
as if the tavern walls themselves were rolling with mirth. She
looked at The Fool, who smiled reassuringly, indicating in the
secret language of performers that she dazzle them some more,
and for all she was worth.

Well, Katy ... That's the girl ... resolved to outrun them,
'Stead of waiting for Death to call her.
She fled fast on her donkey to The Black Cat Mountains,
From whence none have ever returned.

And then something must have half clicked in the brain

of the lead soldier, who stood in front of his comrades in the crowd, barely six feet from Stormy herself. The similarity between the story being told and his task at hand must have suddenly dawned. He banged his staff on the wooden floor and announced, "We search for a girl who murdered a Prince, it is said. And we have orders to 'pprehend her, and any who help her ... So, well, if any of you folks knows anything then, you best be telling us, sharpish like."

Stormy held her breath. The head soldier looked at her directly and asked: "You ever done a gig at her castle, Miss? Over the mountains a way?"

'How old is this girl and what does she look like?'
Said The Fool stepping into the questions.
'She's a princess from the mountains all of thirteen,
But what she looks like we don't have much sense.'

'She ain't been in here, if she's only thirteen,'
Said the Tavernmizz to the head soldier.
'We can' let them in it's county code you see?'
Thus befuddling a man who liked orders.

'Keep your peepers peeled,' spake the soldier.
'She's blonde with blue eyes?' quipped The Fool
'I don't know, Well I've heard ... That's the rumor,'
The soldiers nodded with all in the room.

Asked The Fool in his stride, 'Whence she came? What's

her name?
And how would we know her complexion?'
'Princess Alex Ann Something Some Wilson?'
Said the soldier tackling his brains

'Ahh the rose of the fair skinned Morainian folk.
You construe well this young flibberty-maiden.
I met her once on her birthday I was master of jokes
But am shocked by her crime of passion.'

'These things happen, even to royals, Nay?'
Said the soldier, shaking his brain cells.
'But much better informed we go on our way
So thanks and the Wan God bless y' all.'

The Fool smiled at Stormy and she looked back. Her brown hair, now down to her shoulders where it had shaken free from its plaits, framed her brown eyes, light brown skin, and lips that cracked in a cheeky curve.

It was a strange thing, but The Fool, who knew next to nothing about helping someone deal with shock or guilt, or grief or anything like that, had managed to bring Stormy out of her seemingly impenetrable funk. There, in the glow of the tavern, The Fool had somehow got her feeling something like herself.

Stormy was exhausted beyond exhaustion, light-headed from the ale, and not a little exhilarated from the evening's events. A half-eaten sandwich, some hot goat milk and honey later, the Tavernmizz led Stormy upstairs to bed. In the dim corridor, dark thoughts tried to woo Stormy. But she was able to hold them at bay long enough to get into bed, and collapse into a deep, deep sleep.

Chapter 10
DREAM DREAM DREAM

Deep sleep only lasts so long. The brain, anxious to do its cleaning chores (or worse still, skiving off while its owner is sleeping), has ideas of its own. And thus when the deep sleep became, well, less deep, Stormy entered another world. Strange to say, though, it was the real world, too.

It was dark. She was in *the* cave. She thought that she must have already found the sunshine and pacified the Black Cat. She did not actually remember doing this, but was blinded to this fact by an eager expectation of seeing her father any minute.

There he was. He had his back to her. Her father's body turned, but instead of the warm smile of Walterbald's comforting face, was the anguished look of Mercurio as his head hit the bedpost. Stormy screamed out loud in the dream.

The Fool, who was only half asleep on the other bed, opened his eyes and looked over at the sleeping, dream possessed Princess. His gaze was empathetic, for he knew tragedy and death well. He also knew that even in sleep, escape from troubled thoughts was often only passing. He knew that dream shapes seemed to particularly enjoy feeding on the tormented. Whether they meant to help or hinder, The Fool had never been able to say.

In the dreamscape, Stormy screwed her eyes ever more tightly shut. She dared not open them, but then in dreamtime,

the brain could not care less for the convention of seeing only with open eyes. The specters merely wriggled their way under her eyelids and began their dance anew.

Maybe you've had dreams like this.

Stormy was being chased, uphill. She had run up hills, but not like this. She couldn't see what was pounding up the mountain trail behind her, but she could hear the clatter of hooves and the fierce breathing of animals long extinct. Then the tree line, and the lushness and the smells of the forest suddenly gave way. The grade lessened, and the sky opened up on a plateau of long golden grass so tall, Stormy could barely see above it.

The beasts on her trail forgotten, she now contemplated a new fear: that she was easy prey for the huge black raptor circling above.

A narrow gorge opened in front of Stormy and she stumbled to a halt, all but falling over. And there she beheld a gaggle of *monkeys*, involved in what looked like some well-practiced dance routine.

Hearing her, the monkeys stopped what they were doing, all eyes at once turning towards the stricken girl. As if at some secret signal, the monkeys, seven of them in all, stood on their hind legs and bowed, doffing non-existent caps. Looking at Stormy intently, one over to the left said, "At last. The woebegotten Princess!" At which he and the other six burst into raucous laughter, fell over and rolled in the cleared grass stubble, guffackling incessantly.

"What's the big joke?" she said, but the monkeys kept laughing. Looking at their twisted but unthreatening faces, something clicked in Stormy's brain. She knew. She did not know how she knew, but she *knew* that these were the Giggle Monkeys. Dream logic told her it was of great significance that she'd stumbled upon them.

She woke up in the dark, in a bed in the Grackle Tavern, breathing heavily and thinking desperately that she needed to get back to the dream. But, alas, deep sleep proved to be master this night, pulling Stormy back into dreamless proper rest.

Chapter 11
THE WITCH IN THE DITCH

Stormy and The Fool climbed back into their saddles sometime in the midmorning. They were not as replenished and refreshed as outlaws on the run should have been. The Fool was worse for wear for having stayed up drinking. Stormy also had a mild headache from the beer, and even worse, waves of gut-wrenching stomach pains—like she was missing home, missing her father—even missing Gwynmerelda.

The Fool led them onwards and north out of town, to a break in the forest where yet another mountain trail began to the west.

"So where are we headed now?" asked Stormy

"Why, the Black Cat Mountains, of course," said The Fool.

"You are joking! It's too early for jo-eeughrks ..." Stormy's voice trailed off

The Fool shook his head.

"But no one comes back from the Black Cat Mountains," Stormy said.

The Fool replied, "Only if I'm a no one. Only if you believe the night tales. I've been back and forth, ooh a dozen times since I was a kid, I guess."

"But how?"

"Because I know the way."

"And the Black Cat of legend?"

"Never seen it."

"Oh," said Stormy. She didn't mention that she had seen it. Even if it was only in a dream, Stormy knew it was really real. "How long will it take to get there?"

"Could be a day or two, depending on who we meet along the way."

"That sounds ominous."

"It probably won't be."

They rode on in silence for some time, and Stormy's thoughts began to wander. She tried not to think about what had happened at Bald Mountain Castle, but then Bald Mountain had been her home for thirteen summers. It was her whole life. Her stomach groaned again. The few times she had left Morainia on family trips, they had generally headed south, occasionally to Rockport and the ocean, to visit her Unkle Jude and her sort-of-cousins. Sometimes she went on business trips with her father to meet with the kings and queens of southern kingdoms. She had never really been any distance north, where they were headed now.

The north beyond Morainia was mainly mountainous, with occasional small and isolated communities. To the north of that was the legendary Ice Wall itself, a frozen wasteland going on forever to the top of the world, for all anybody knew. She shivered when she thought of it. And who wouldn't?

A good passage of the sun later, The Fool announced, "Stream crossing up ahead. We should stop and rest, and eat."

By the edge of a burbling crick, still flush with snowmelt,

The Fool delved into his saddlebag. He passed Stormy a crust of not-too-stale bread and some goat cheese in wax paper.

"Whyrrewe?" said Stormy, her mouth too full to form the words"

"Come again?" said The Fool.

"I mean why are we going this way, and where are we headed? Are we just going to keep going forever? What's the plan?"

"Ahh! I was wondering when you were going to ask that."

"There is a plan. Isn't there?"

"Well sort of," said The Fool as he rummaged once more in the saddlebag.

"What do you mean sort of? We're headed towards the ice sheet, where people die. We're running away, but where to? What's going to happen?"

"That last I can't answer. But I can tell you why we are headed this way."

"Well why?"

"We are looking for the Black Bird."

"What?" Stormy said, startled. But before she could say anything else, a loud cracking voice stopped them in their tracks.

"Well pluck my boggerworts at crizeymas," the voice exclaimed, "If it isn't Dickemmy Fool! The Black Bird told me you was coming, but I didn't half believe him."

Stormy and The Fool both turned in the direction of the voice, toward a small rise in the woods, a little upstream from where they sat. The Fool smiled.

Stormy looked at him, perplexed, then back to where the voice had come from. There was a sound of cracking twigs underfoot. First one head, and then a second appeared over the rise as two women came towards them.

The older one whispered something to the younger as they approached, then stopped suddenly, the younger girl bumping into her. The crone stooped, stared through scrunched up eyes, and let out a loutish cackle.

The Fool laughed.

"Er— do you all know each other?" asked Stormy, stunned.

"Well, we did. And more than once if I remember," rasped the old woman, setting off another cackle. "Right good fun it was, too."

The Fool, still grinning widely, bowed with a flourish. "Let me introduce you to The Witch in the Ditch."

"A real witch?" said Stormy excitedly. She had always wanted to see one.

"You see a ditch don't you?" scowled the old woman. "Well, my little chumpkin. Then that's where you will find The Witch in the Ditch." She spread her arms, as if indicating she owned everything around.

Stormy did not see a ditch, but didn't think the woman would take kindly to her pointing this out.

"Haven't met my daughter have you? Glamour, say hello to The Fool."

The much younger woman stepped forward.

The Fool approached to shake the hand she offered, but he

suddenly hesitated, looking at The Witch.

"She isn't …?"

"No you old birch-barker. She ain't that old, are you, Glam?"

The girl, a few summers older than Stormy, smiled and shook The Fool's outstretched hand for him.

"'Iziemas, it really has been a long time, Fool. And you are?" said the crone to Stormy.

"I , I am The Fool's apprentice," said Stormy, not sure that they should trust anyone.

"Well tell us a jekkler then, Fool's apprentice."

Stormy looked at The Fool. The Fool nodded.

"I—I. Oh! I know one. Which followed who? The chicken or the egg?"

"I dunno," offered The Witch: "To get to the other side?"

"No. The Witch came first, and who cares about the chicken or the egg after that."

Glamour burst out laughing. The Fool allowed himself a wry smile, while The Witch in the Ditch looked perplexed. Then she let off another screek as if she had gotten the joke and accepted the compliment.

"Whatever, Fool's apprentice. I expect you and old Sagack here will be wanting some tea? Unhitch yer donks and follow me."

The Witch fell in with The Fool, and led them over the slight rise. Stormy winced from the pain in her stomach. Glamour offered her a hand.

"You all right?"

73

"Just a gutache."

"You have done well, sick and all," said the raven-haired lateen in an admiring voice.

Stormy looked puzzled.

"I mean getting so far away from Morainia without being caught."

"How did you kno—" Stormy stopped, not wanting to give herself away any more.

"It's okay. We're friends." Glamour smiled. "I met you when you was a baby, down in Morainia. You won't remember that. But me ma knew who you was soon as we set eyes on you."

"Yes, but I meant more the bit about us not being caught?"

"Oh, my mother. She sees things."

"Witch powers?" asked Stormy, excited.

"Naw. She has a bad habit of intercepting message birds and reading all about other people's business. She saw the note your mother sent to King Walterbald."

"What?"

"Not to worry. She petted it, fed it, and sent it on its way again. More likely to get to where it's going really. But me ma has always been a nosey boggler. It serves her well. It helps her do her witch stuff."

They came to a clearing, and there was an old cabin set back towards the trees. All along the front was a most impractically placed ditch. A rickety wooden gangplank led the way across to the front door.

Inside the cabin it was dark. Glamour busied herself lighting the kero-lamps, and the yellow glow welcomed the travelers in.

Stormy hovered.

"Sit down, sit down," beckoned the young woman, but Stormy felt her gaze drawn to the back wall, where a series of oil paintings hung.

The four paintings, mostly dark, especially in the half-light, depicted various creatures. Familiar yet not familiar, like in her own dreams, but not quite the same as her own dreams: The Black Cat, at the mouth of a cave, older and wiser looking, with a glint in its eye. A huge black bird with penetrating red eyes. And then a gaggle of ape-like creatures stood around a fire engaged in some ritual.

The last painting was different. It showed a huge silver-streaked creature. It could have been a bird or a giant sea-ray, or something else altogether. The creature was wedged between a cleft in the mountains, suggesting it was huge beyond measure. It looked flopped down stuck, but with satisfied eyes, as if it were panting for breath at the end of a long journey. Via its lolling red tongue descended adults and children, seemingly being delivered to the earth.

Stormy looked at Glamour asking the question with her eyes ...

"The Mothshark," affirmed the older girl.

Stormy pointed at them excitedly, "Have you seen these monsters?"

"My forebears knew them. Something of my ancestors is in me, so I see them in my mindeye. Then I paint them."

"I see them too!"

"Maybe the night tales from when you were young work

75

their magic in your mind."

"Then they're real!"

"Of course they're real. Only silly people think the old stories aren't true."

Stormy studied the pictures. "The Fool says we are looking for the Black Bird," she said slowly.

"If the Black Bird wants to see you, then I am sure you will see him. My mother exchanges stories with him. She tells me the stories, and I see him in my dreams."

"He talks to her?"

"Either that or my mother drank too much mushroom tea."

The two girls giggled together, and then a look of pain crossed Stormy's face.

"Ohhh," Glamour said with a knowing intake of breath. "I see what's wrong. Come on. We'll fix you up."

Confused, Stormy followed her to the kitchen, the pain still gripping her gut.

Glamour looked back at her reassuringly. "It's the best time, you know, the time between one thing and another—the best time to get your fortune told."

"What time? What other?"

But Glamour didn't answer, just led her to a flop seat by the woodstove, where The Witch and The Fool teased each other over a boiling kettle.

"What will it be?" The Witch asked.

"Oooh, I could murder a good cup of tea," said The Fool.

The Witch laughed uproariously.

"Same old Fool," she said fondly. "Tea it is all round. And then I will read the fortune of Madame Princess 'Prentice here."

Stormy looked ill at ease.

The Witch in the Ditch busied herself making tea, and Glamour handed Stormy a cup.

Stormy blew on the tea and skimmed off a few drops with an intake of breath. The tea tasted bitter.

Glamour smiled and whispered. "It'll help with your cramps."

Stormy took another gulp and felt her insides warm.

She felt safe. And The Witch looked different now. She looked friendly. Kind.

"Now, Princess. You come sit beside me. Shift your bony ass, Fool. Make way for the Princess."

Stormy hesitated. Glamour smiled at her reassuringly.

"Leave some leaves in the bottom of yer cup, Princess."

The Witch took hold of Stormy's free hand and turned her palm skywards, uncurling her fingers flat. Her touch was bony and scaly and felt very old, but was surprisingly warm.

"Long Life," mused The Witch. Letting go of Stormy's hand and taking the cup from her other hand, The Witch commanded silence without any outward sign of communication.

She took the cup in both of her hands and looked into it, like it was a deep well, adjusting her eyes to the darkness to be able to see the bottom.

"Ooooohh, oooooohh." The Witch smiled, but this time it was not what you would call a comforting smile.

"Oooh. Ha ha ha."

What? What is it? Stormy was saying inside her own head, but not daring to interrupt.

The Witch looked for what seemed like long moments, but was probably a series of short moments. She grimaced and grunted, and Stormy felt herself tense even more, beads of sweat breaking her scalp.

Stormy looked at The Fool who cracked a half smile. She looked to Glamour again for reassurance.

After a seeming eternity, The Witch looked up and let out another raucous laugh.

Stormy couldn't help it. She said, "What? What is it?"

"Three dead princes!" spat The Witch. "I see three dead princes."

At which the Princess looked at her, appalled.

The room spun. Had there been something in the tea? Stormy closed her eyes, swaying to keep her balance, and opened them again to see Glamour and The Fool looking at her with concern. The Witch eyed her narrowly.

"Ah," The Witch said. "I see what it is. The moonblood time. Better get her to bed, Glamour."

"What?" Stormy said, startled and dizzy. "Blood? What blood?" She fell heavily into the chair and felt something wet between her legs. When she looked down, there was a stain of dark red spreading on the edge of her poncho. And then she didn't know any more, because she fainted dead away.

Chapter 12
GIRLTALK

When Stormy awoke she was in a warm bed. She felt a coarse towel under her butt, but the rest of the sheets were soft. Opening her eyes she saw Glamour come into focus, smiling, and felt the warmth of the lateen's hand on her own forehead.

"What happened to me?"

"You are having your first moonblood."

"I'm blood-cursed," sobbed Stormy, not listening. "The Witch said I would kill two more princes! I don't want to kill anyone!"

"Ssshh," Glamour said, dabbing at her head with a damp cloth that smelled of lavender. "First things first. You are only cursed in so far as all women are cursed. Your bleeding. It means that your body is changing from a girl into woman. Didn't your mother tell you?"

At this Stormy was silent for a moment. Then, finally, she said, "Am I dying?"

Glamour laughed, but not unkindly. "No. Unless ... well, I guess you are, in a way. At least, the child in you is dying. And the adult is being born. The blood's a sign of it."

Stormy looked mortified.

"It's a good sign. All women have it. It means you're healthy. Some moons it's not so bad. Most girls I know are in tune with the full moon. It's your body cleansing itself, so you'll have a fresh egg inside you, when it is time. And if you fall in love with a handsome prin— ." The words died on Glamour's lips.

Stormy howled and smothered herself into the pillow, but the soft down could not prevent her being tortured anew by the mental picture of the dead, decaying, and most decidedly not handsome Mercurio.

Glamour stood. "I'll bring you something. I'll. I—. Don't worry … I won't be long." And Glamour left the room knowing she needed The Witch's help.

Back in the sitting room, The Fool was speaking in serious tones.

"Do you think you can summon him by tomorrow?"

"Maybe," said The Witch. "He don't usually pay me any heed, but we are looking dark times in the teeth. He knows which side his turkabird is basted. And he's been looking for you hisself. He wants to meet the girl."

The Fool was about to respond, when Glamour ducked under the drape leading from the back of the cabin.

"What is it, missy?" said The Witch to her daughter.

"You shouldn't have told her fortune."

"You know me. Whatever is pressing in my brain has to have wings."

"Yes, but you've upset her something fierce."

"It'll work out for the best. Now, you be needing a stronger potion by the look on your mug."

The Witch shuffled over to the wall and drew back a curtain, revealing an old apothecary, crafted from yellow wood and fashioned into row upon row of tiny fist-sized drawer fronts.

"Witchgirl! Help your old mother out. Top row. Third from the morningsun."

Glamour grabbed the stool and scaled the apothecary. From above her head she fished out a leather pouch and tossed it towards the table. On a reflex, The Fool plucked it out of the air, raised it to his nostrils and, nodding his head approvingly, handed it to The Witch.

"It's very mild," said Glamour, handing Stormy the pipe.

"Will it put me to sleep?" Stormy asked hopefully, and then frowning, "Will it make me have bad dreams?"

"No, no! None of that. It'll just relax you. And then we can talk without all freaking out on each other. Just do as I did."

Stormy brought the pipe to her mouth and inhaled deeply, which sent her into a coughing fit.

"Easy, girl," laughed Glamour. "Pass it back to me. And watch me closely this time. Inhale gently. Let the vapors wash over you."

Stormy tried again with less coughing.

"Ere, shufty up a bit." Stormy wriggled on her back sideways and Glamour lay down alongside her on the bed.

"Now just lie down, close your eyes and relax. Think warm thoughts. You are lying in a boat, floating down a river with a wide gentle current on a summer afternoon."

The two girls were silent, apart from the rise and fall of their shallow breathing. They lay there for some measureless amount of time.

Stormy felt a smile spread across her face, and made a whimper trying to stifle it. It was no use. The giggle erupted mostly from her nostrils and the bed shook.

"What?"

"I—," and Stormy broke into a full laugh. A whole array of muscles across her face danced a dance of joy, for being allowed to do again what they did best. "Leaves," she said. "We floated under a tree and the leaves from a drooping branch tickled my nose."

Glamour guffawed. "What are you talking about, girl? I was being massaged by the river spirit. He was just about to move from my shoulders to my neck when you interrupted."

Stormy laughed even louder. "River spirit? You've never seen a river spirit!"

"Have too."

"In your dreams," said the Princess, now not fearing dreams at all.

"Yes. In my dreams."

"What's he like?"

"He's strong and handsome. And he has a cute goat beard. Not like the shaggy mess all the boys are wearing these days."

Stormy was silent at this, thinking thoughts that surprised even her. She was even more surprised when she heard herself say, "You ever been with a boy?"

Glamour almost seemed to be expecting the question. "Yes," she said calmly. "And more than once, too."

"What's it like?" Stormy said, raising herself up on to an

elbow so she could see Glamour's face.

"Well, at first I didn't like it. But that's because I didn't like the boy. Though I didn't know that at the time. I thought I loved him."

"Eugghh!" spat Stormy, shaking at the memory of looking longingly at Mercurio when they were banqueting at Bald Mountain.

"Then I met this other boy and I didn't really fancy him, but we got drunk and started fooling around. And he was the sweetest most loving boy you could hope to meet. And it felt good. Really good." Glamour reached for the herb pipe, lost for a moment in her own sweeter memories.

Stormy had a warm flash, thinking of when she had kissed River, the traveling player. Then she thought of Fred and winced.

"So what happened?"

"Well," Glamour shrugged sadly. "I didn't fancy him. I mean in the morning when I woke up."

"Oh," said Stormy, now thoroughly confused.

"I once slept with a girl too. Same thing. I went with the flow and it was okay, but not my ... I dunno. It just wasn't me. Ohh, but she was heartbroken. Poor thing."

"I don't think I will ever fancy anyone again," Stormy said. "After what happened to me."

Glamour passed her the smoke. "You will, girl. There's no magic way to find out. I mean find out who you are. It happens or it doesn't. You try things along the way, 'cos it's part of seeing whether you really like someone or not. It can feel really weird, or great, or all mixed up at the same time. It's not easy to know

if it's right or wrong. It's just part of finding out who you are."

"It sounds painful to me," said Stormy.

The girls were silent for a moment.

"You learned the first rule though," said Glamour.

"What's that?"

"Well if someone forces themselves on you it's always wrong. No matter who it is! Mind you. I don't know if I'd be brave enough to kill a fella, even if he were a bastard gropeller."

The girls looked into each other's eyes, uncertain of where the words had led them, when a gentle cramp in Stormy's stomach burst softly, combusting into a laugh, and the girls fell on the bed together, howling helplessly.

Which is how those moments go, sometimes. And a good thing, too.

A little later when the seriousness that had been scattered to the four winds was beginning to recombine, Stormy asked cautiously, "Was that a prophecy? I mean, what your mother said."

"It might be nothing. She didn't say *you* killed the princes."

"That's what she meant though. Wasn't it?"

"She said you had a long life-line, so maybe all it means is that some of the princes you meet in the summers and summers to come will die before you do. I mean, you know what princes are like. Even the good ones. Always tempting fate, trying to beat their fathers and impress the girls. Must be something in their blood."

Stormy thought of her father, who was Wangodknowswhere. He was no longer a prince, but she feared for him all the same.

Chapter 13
SORTOFINGTON

Stormy never got up from the bed to go pee or anything. She drifted off to sleep after Glamour had gently undressed her, changed her bloodsheet, and tucked her into bed. She kissed Stormy on the forehead, but even a kiss from a true friend can offer only so much protection.

It was not until the dead of night, when Stormy really did need to pee, that she woke.

It felt strange, to be in another new house. It was even stranger to feel the weight of forces that had ripped her world apart. It was only three nights ago that her father had tucked her up in her own bed. Now her home seemed like it was a gadzillion miles away, and her old life lost on a distant planet.

She shivered as she got back into bed, pulled the sheet close around her, and slowly sort-of-drifted off.

The dreamland of Sortofington was not where she wanted to be. But Sortofington was where her troubled mind looked for answers. We have all been there.

The Giggle Monkeys were there, laughing. Always laughing. Singing and laughing all at the same time.

Princess, Princess,
I bet you won't remember this.
Take a good long look

For goodness sake.

Princess, Princess,
I bet you won't remember this.
Wish upon the sun,
When you wake.

Princess, Princess,
I bet you won't …

"Okay, okay. I get the picture," stormed Stormy in her dream.

The Giggle Monkeys looked at her dumbfounded, then slowly resumed chattering among themselves. The monkey with a gray streak of hair running back from his forehead in a mohawk stepped forward.

"I am Gimminy Giggle. You are the honorary Princess Giggle. And we are giving you the tools to do the job."

"Tools? What tools? What Job? I don't see any tools!"

"Well," said Gimminy Giggle, "that depends on what happens next."

"So what does happen next?"

"We won't know until it happens, you see …"

"So how can you give me the right tools?" pleaded Stormy, exasperated.

"We can't be sure," said Gimminy. "But what we have given you should stand you in good stead when the time comes."

"But you haven't given me anything!"

"We have too! We gave her the tools, didn't we lads?" Gimminy appealed to his comrades.

Now the Giggle Monkeys muttered among themselves again.

"Well, if she can't remember it in a dream, then my bet is as good as won," said Garama Giggle.

"Don't count your gracklechicks!" said Gimminy Giggle.

"I think she has hidden depths," said Goandermi Giggle.

"Time she met the Bird," said Garama.

You may think all this talk and pictures of strange creatures was only legend. Or maybe it is mere pretendsuppose to scare children at night? It's easy to forget that the night stories we tell our children are simply less scary versions of the tales adults tell each other. It's easy to forget that our ancestors fought monsters. And some lived to tell the tale.

Admittedly the strangest creature we have actually seen thus far in Stormy's waking world is a donkey. But that is about to change. For there in the distance, in the alive world, just below the dawn horizon, where the ice sheet stretches out forever, there comes a black speck. Impossible to tell at this distance what it is, but the very fact we can see it at all means it is bigger than anything we have previously known.

Back in the dream, the Giggle Monkeys still talked among themselves.

"Time she met the Bird," the whole said as one.

"That's you, Miss Princess," chimed Goandermi. "Now don't forget."

Which bird? Forget what? mouthed Stormy, as she slid from Sortofington into a deeper untroubled sleep ...

Chapter 14
THE BLACK BIRD

"What's that?" said The Fool, rubbing his eyes and pulling himself up on the couch bed.

"I said, it really is time she met the Bird," said an exasperated Witch in the Ditch. "I just coaxed a message bird down, see? Comes from Bald Mountain, but it tells news from King Jude in Rockport."

"What news?" said The Fool, shaking himself awake.

"The Oosarians! They have an army of boats up the north coast sailing beyond Rockport. They will soon be sailing up the mouth of the Lumbiana, he says. Powered by slaves, he says. Wance they reach River Bald Falls they—"

"Boats. Boats. What boats?" gasped The Fool.

"They're like floating cities, says Jude. Five hundred fighting men on each of 'em. Quare creatures makes up many of their number. He says there's ten ships. No one's ever dreamed it. Gwynmerelda says … it's all addressed to Walterbald of course. She says he has to get his ass back there as fast as he can fart."

The Fool was wide awake now. Glamour came into the room, rubbing her eyes. "What's all the ruckus? It's barely past sun up."

"Mergnecy in Morainia," howled her mother. "Go wake the girl."

Stormy was asleep, but not for long.

"You mean the Oosarians are about to invade Morainia? But, but how? Why?" clamored Stormy, clutching her mug of tea. "It's all my fault isn't it?" she burst out. "For killing that stupid Prince! And I didn't mean to!" she wailed.

But then she stopped. The thought came to her: It was *his* fault. *I might not like it but I can't undo what I've done.* From which it will be seen that Stormy was indeed changing.

"Well, there be another prince or two on them warships, no doubt," quipped The Witch.

"Mother!" Glamour said, looking at Stormy. She sat beside the Princess, put a comforting arm around her, and gave The Witch a disparaging look.

"No, it's okay, thanks," Stormy said grimly to her friend. But she squeezed her hand as she said it.

The Fool stood up and began pacing. "This has nothing to do with you, other than the fact that you are Morainian. The *why* is simple. Since as long as we can remember, Oosarian rulers have eyed Morainia's metal reserves jealously."

"Hah!" interrupted The Witch. "They be jealous, is why! Never met an Oosarian who could stand to see someone else having a good time. That Mercurio was bad enough. But them other two, his brothers, Toromos and Braggardio, are war wolves to be sure." Her eyes narrowed.

"Nukeander and Mercurio, and the courtship deal was a ploy," spat The Fool. It was all a diversion, while the war fleet sailed north." He laughed, but there was a proud look in his eye. "Didn't know they'd get *you*, though, did they, Alexandra Stormybald Wilson?"

Stormy frowned. "We have to find my dad!"

"I sent out word already," squawked The Witch. As if on cue, a bird flew into the half-open front door, clattering across the floor in a scuff of feathers.

It was a humble message bird, smaller than a hen. The poor thing looked exhausted. The Witch scuttled over to relieve the bird of its burden, lifting it on to the counter where a bowl of water waited. After the bird had gulped bird-sized gulps, The Witch untied the note wrapped around its leg, and unrolling it, read aloud:

> *Keep your hair on, comrades. Eat a good breakfast. That is very important. I will be with you before it has settled.*

"It's signed 'M'," cooed The Witch.

"Holy Joke!" ennunced The Fool. "Has the Bird ever come down the Mountain to visit upon anyone?"

Stormy looked perplexed.

"I mean wan has to go and find the Bird. He doesn't come to you," explained The Fool.

"Is he on his way, Ma?" said Glamour with strange excitement. "Really? Truly?"

"I never knowed it before, but that's what he says," said The Witch.

To Stormy's surprise, Glamour blushed. But she avoided her friend's eye, and bustled about making breakfast.

The next moments were filled with breakfast and speculation. Time passed slowly. But in the time it takes to cook up some eggs, eat them, and have a second cup of tea—in the time it would have taken that cup of tea to cool were it not drunk still hot, a shadow crossed the eastern window.

All in the room heard the beating of giant wings outside.

"You'd better come out," said a voice in a deep bass growl. "I wouldn't take kindly to ruffling my feathers on your hovelposts."

Stormy, who was nearest the door, led the four of them into the warming mountain sunlight, and there, preening his enormously long feathers, stood the Black Bird.

"Fool. Witch, and you must be Stormy? My, you have grown. And you are?"

"Glamour, sir!" said The Witch's daughter, blushing again. To her surprise, and even with other things to think about, Stormy suddenly saw that her friend had a crush on the giant Bird.

And why wouldn't she? Standing some twelve or more feet tall, the Black Bird looked part grackle, part raven, part raptor, and part handsome devil. Unusually, however this bird had teeth, which made its giant beak very severe looking.

On each foot, his dangerously sharp talons were made up of three forward-facing claws, and a fourth opposable thumb-claw. Each claw was the girth of a man's thigh. And just when it seemed the bird could impose his presence no more, he flared his feather *pants*. Hunching his shoulders back so the wing tips crossed behind him, he looked all the more regal.

The bird was indeed black. Black feathers, black beak, black legs … black mouth lining as he opened his beak wide, yawning.

93

But his eyes were different. The milky white-ish nictating membrane that protected them masked a brilliant fiery red ring around black pupils. Then the strangest thing happened. The bird blinked, and his third eyelid rolled back revealing those red eyes. With a birdish shake of the head, the vivid red faded, revealing a more natural looking brown, with unusually bright eye-whites. Shocking as this sudden transformation was, it gave the bird an altogether mellower and more approachable appearance.

It was, in truth, a most staggeringly noble-looking Bird.

"Just shaking the flight-sight," he said to no one in particular. As if flexing that brain inside its massive head, the Black Bird shook his crown and bowed toward Stormy.

"Hmmm," he said, "you have a look of your mother."

Stormy bowed back. "You, who you … You know me?" she stammered.

"Ah yes. But first you should know me. I am, in no particular order, the Black Bird, Black Beak, Red Eyes, Wolf-Bird, known to my friends as Emmeur, or M for short. Scientically as—well, my kind defies the usual classifications—so most people call me The Gricklegrack. The grackle part is scientically a misnomer, but it stuck. I was a good friend of your mother, and through her I became friends with your father. You won't remember, but I met you when you were two winters old."

Stormy didn't remember, and even if she had, the idea that this monster, majestic as he was, had been friends with her mother was more stunning. "You knew my mother?" said Stormy dreamily. And then, like it was pushing off from the bottom of a deep pool, a more urgent thought broke the surface bursting for breath: "Do you know where my dad is?"

"Yes and yes. Yes, your mother was the bravest young woman I have ever known, and I hope for no less from her daughter." At this, the Black Bird looked sternly at Stormy, who immediately straightened her back.

He gave her a look of qualified approval. "And yes, I know where your father is. I've come to take you to him."

"Oh oh," The Fool whistled. But the Black Bird turned a quelling eye his way, and he was still.

"First ...," the Bird went on.

"But what about my dad?" bawled Stormy, stepping forward.

"Stormy. Before bravery comes wisdom. And before both comes patience."

Stormy took a breath, stepped back, and the Bird nodded his approval again.

"I have brought something of the greatest importance," the Bird explained, "to leave here in safety until we can return for it in happier times. After it is safely bestowed, then we'll go to your father."

At this, Stormy, The Witch, and Glamour looked perplexed. The bird plainly was not carrying anything with him.

Stormy found herself moving sideways and looking around behind him, but still nothing. And as she did so, the huge bird squatted slightly, as if he were about to do his business. The feathers around his eyes and face formed the faintest of grimaces, as if showing the business in progress. It was a mark of his great strength of personality that all of this looked quite natural, and not funny at all, as it might have looked if you or I tried it.

"My undercarriage," said the Bird, answering an unasked question.

A moment later, emerging from below his probber's nose came a sphere, which became an ovaloid, which became an egg as it fell onto the dirt. The Bird shuffled gracefully around, scraping a shallow hole in the dirt with one talon. The Gricklegrack stood the egg upright with a deft movement of his other talon. The egg was about three feet tall and looked like a gray-blue rock. Old and pockmarked as it was, at some time it evidently had an overall sheen, a few traces of which remained.

"Aaaghhhh!" The Witch hissed.

"Whaaatizzit?" chorused Glamour and The Fool.

"The Egg of Geddon," cried The Witch. "It spells doom."

"Mother! Don't be so melodramatic."

"It is in the prophecy!"

"Which prophecy? If you could keep track of all the prophecies you have made, been party to, or read about, we wouldn't be able to turn over a stone without fear of unleashing every volcanemon that ever spouted fire into the air! Honestly!"

"The Egg of Geddon was in your father's leaves," said The Witch, turning a staring eye upon Stormy. "'Tis said the creature who will be hatched is all knowing, all seeing, and wiser than the Ancient Ones. 'Tis said the creature within will eat the world!"

Glamour looked a little more interested now, while Stormy was beginning to see The Witch as a serial harbinger of doom and gloom, in a world that could not possibly get much worse.

With all attention on the egg, The Gricklegrack resumed its crouch and, from a secret hiding place, brought out a plain wooden box, which clattered on the ground. The Bird drummed his left talon rhythmically on the box while he waited for the bickering to peter out.

"I have a double harness in here," he said, still drumming on the box. "It won't be comfortable, but it will do the job."

At this, The Fool groaned. "I knew it," he muttered. "My fear of heights won't stand this!"

The Bird ignored him.

"I leave the egg here, Witch, in your good hands.""

"No! No! Nooooo!" wailed The Witch.

"Walterbald found this egg moons ago and he gave it to me, to see if I could crack its mystery."

The Fool groaned again.

"No pun intended." The Bird gave a slow smile, and Glamour clapped her hands. Gazing at him, she gave a deep sigh.

"But, why are we even bothering with this egg, if it even is an egg," interjected Stormy. "Aren't we losing precious time? What about my dad?"

"Indeed," cawed, The Gricklegrack. "But patience again, Princess. All this concerns your father."

"Speaking, like your father, as a scientic," he went on,

looking directly with his nearest eye into Stormy's own, "this egg is made of a substance we have never encountered. It is hard, yet relatively lightweight. Your father and I tried to —er, hatch it. I sat on it for a whole month last winter."

"Ych, but what would you know about hatching eggs?" The Fool objected.

"We do have birds up north on the Great Ice Wall where the male protects and hatches the egg."

"Oh," said The Fool, nonplussed.

"Then I dropped it from five feet high, ten feet, twenty feet, and so on. There are little dings you will see. The only sign of a crack is the horizontal line running around the top. That was there when Walterbald found it. You see my claw marks where I tried to pry it open. Nothing!"

Stormy went over to the egg and put her hands upon it. It wasn't cold but it wasn't warm either. She crouched down beside it and put her ear against it.

"Nothing," she said

"No matter," said the great Bird. And at this, he drew himself up to his fullest and most impressive height, causing Glamour to give a little squeal in spite of herself.

"I am the guardian of the egg. I carried it here, but there is dangerous work ahead. Under the circumstances it is proper that I assure the egg's safekeeping by leaving it with another member of the Order." He gave The Witch a gimlet-eyed look.

"But I'm not IN the Order," howled The Witch.

"Kneel," commanded the Bird in the kind of tone that assured obedience. Rolling her eyes, The Witch somewhat creakily obeyed.

"He's not going to smash that egg on her head, is he? He'll break her skull!" muttered The Fool.

"Glamour," crooned the Bird.

"Sir!" said Glamour, completely entranced.

"Call me M."

"Mmmmmm," she hummmmed dreamily.

"Glamour. Be a flame and bring me an egg."

Glamour disappeared back into the cabin.

"Probably just a foul-smelling rotten egg," said The Fool to The Witch, nodding at the large egg.

The Witch looked up at him, thoroughly uncomfortable. "Can I get up yet?" she hacked.

"Be patient," said the Bird. "Ah, Glamour. Would you do the honors?"

"With pleasure," Glamour replied, reappearing with a brown hen's egg.

"Witch," spoke the Bird, "I hereby appoint you into the Order, the first woman—"

"Second," said Stormy.

"Second? Oh, of course," said the Bird, gracefully acknowledging his error. "I hereby appoint you, Witch in the Ditch, into the Order of the Accidental Adventurers."

At which point Glamour cracked the hen's egg on her mother's crown.

The Witch in the Ditch howled as if she were mortally wounded, but she was cut short by the great Bird: "As I stand here, I swear by the Order. I swear by all who stand here upon this egg." He lay a talon upon the egg. "I swear that we shall return to you, Witch and Glamour, with Walterbald, his daughter, and my friend The Fool. And together we shall crack the mystery of the egg."

"But my father? Can we go to my father now? Can we? ..."

"Yes," said the Bird gravely. "I need help with the harness."

"I'll do it!" Glamour said, tripping over the wooden box that held it in her hurry to get to the Bird.

"And then we'll fly," the Bird said. "You and me and ..."

"No," groaned The Fool. He was airsick already.

"And The Fool."

"I was afraid you would say that."

Stormy gazed at the Bird, as Glamour cooed and fitted the harness in place on his broad, feathered back. The Princess's breath caught in her throat. Was it true? Would she—could she—really fly? But to fly, that was something the Wangod had forbidden the people of the world. It was in the *Book of Life.* To fly was the work of the Devanimals.

The Bird gave her a slow, almost lazy, look, as if he could read her mind. And then—it must have been in answer—one of his eyes gave a long, luxurious wink.

Stormy knew it was true. She didn't care what the probbers said. She would fly. And she would find her father when she did.

Chapter 15
THE DEVANIMALS' WORK

Even in a sort-of-fairy tale world, it defied belief that a bird of such size could ever get off the ground.

More perplexing still, how could the Bird not only talk, but also clearly think as humans did? Maybe, even better than most humans did. You may also be wondering, whether 'tis true that The Gricklegrack can out-grackle a whole swarm of its distant blackbird relatives, corvus, quiscalus, or otherwise? Without yet having heard his war-caw, we cannot say.

But all these things suddenly seemed less impossible when you were a few thousand feet up in the air. For Stormy and The Fool were strapped in tight, side-by-side, to the Bird's back. Within the strap arrangements they each had what looked like down-filled sleeping bags, to shield them from the cold.

You could say the flight was uneventful. That is, compared to the preceding four days and nights, nothing much untoward happened. But uneventful as it might have been, to Stormy the views and in-flight entertainment were brainfryingly exhilarating.

Everything about that day would be etched forever in Stormy's memory. Seeing the tear in Glamour's eye through her own tears after kissing her goodbye. Being harnessed in by deer-hide straps. Seeing The Gricklegrack's eyes turn back to that chilling red. Feeling every bone-shaking footfall as the giant bird moved from standing to a breakneck run. Finally—as the huge black wings began to flap with a powerful rhythmic beating—the momentum that lifted them smoothly into the air, and the altogether new feeling of no longer being earthbound.

The world looked different from above. To the east, for Stormy was on the right side of The Gricklegrack's back as they headed due north, were the towering Mezzala Ice Mountains. In school, in books, Stormy had learned that no humans had ever traversed these mountains. Popular wisdom said the mountains stretched thousands of miles to the east, to where the land dropped to a wasteland and fell into the sea.

But from a bird's eye-view, it was very different. Stormy could make out a distant forest landscape, similar to the one they were now flying directly above. She could see for herself that while the mountains were vast, stretching as far as the eye could see north to south, they were relatively narrow from west to east. There was even a great green valley that took out a big chunk of the mountains on the eastern side.

Stormy looked directly down for the merest of moments before her stomach told her to keep looking forward. She saw the lower mountainsides of fir trees by the millions, where each looked like the smallest individual tuft of pine needles on a single branch.

"Oh oh oh," said The Fool, "I can't look down." Stormy could hear him faintly over the whooshing air.

"It's so beautiful! I could cry with joy!" shouted back Stormy.

"Don't." The Fool advised at the top of his lungs. "Your

103

tears will freeze."

Then there was a deep gurgling sound, as the Bird cleared his throat.

With only their heads peeping out of the flight-sacks, by pressing their respective ears against the soft feathers of The Gricklegrack's neck, Stormy and The Fool could hear what he was saying over the rush of the wind.

"See the clouds," said The Gricklegrack. "We will head that direction." And as the Bird banked to the west, The Fool let out a shrill, sledblastering shriek.

These sort-of-fairy-tale clouds, sunlit, fluffy, and white against the vast blue sky, were of course no such thing when the Bird actually hit them. As they dropped into the clouds, moist wisps became a dense, gray-green mist. Then shafts of light from above stabbed into the fog. And suddenly they were through the white billowy mattress, so beguiling to the eye.

And then, there it was. As white as a dream, as beautiful and as forbidding. There at the edge of the mountains, it ran jagged and free all the way west to the sea. North, it went on forever: the Great Ice Wall.

"I can't look," The Fool wailed. But Stormy, as the Black Bird swung first this way, then that in the cold currents of air, stared down, entranced. The Great Ice Wall! She was the first girl ever to see it! It was no story! What other fairy tales had she been told, that were actually as true as true could be?

And Stormy remembered something from a dream. She remembered being upset by the notion that people were alive *during* the cataclysm. She remembered a large upright, sort-of-monkey-looking man, explaining it all to her and then laughing. She thought of Glamour's paintings. And then there was something about tools?

"But there weren't any people before the dark times," thought Stormy as if reciting a school lesson. "And how could there have been any *talking* animals? Animals don't—."

Then it hit Stormy. She was flying. Something she would have thought utterly impossible as recently as that morning at breakfast. Likewise, she was in the company of a giant talking Bird, who was not only sentient but, thus far, showed a very human-like emotional warmth.

All of this Princess Stormy had been taught was clearly impossible. But here she was. What else that was impossible was actually, positively, possible?

She wanted to ask The Gricklegrack if he was alive before or during the dark times. Maybe his forbears were alive, and they were the ones who fell afoul of the Wangod?

She yearned to find her father, and to sit with him and ask him question after question. He had always encouraged her curiosity—not like some of the probbers who catechized her at lessons, answering any question sternly with the words, "That is the way it is. That is the way it always has been."

Here above the tree line, above the expanse of ice as far as the eye could see, the lessons of her childhood seemed very far away. What new lessons she would learn next, when they found her dad at work?

But when they landed, delicately, on a ridge of ice next to the small opening of a cave, her father wasn't there.

They found signs of a struggle. Tools strewn here and there.

And a patch of bright red blood in the snow.

Stormy shrieked, jumped from her place in the harness, and ran to it.

"Not human blood," said The Fool, tipping himself from his harness. He knew that right away.

The Gricklegrack stared at the scene impassively. Impossible to read the great Bird's thoughts.

"The tracks are all wrong," The Fool said rapidly, forgetting his airsickness in his heartsickness at the scene before him. "Two sets, and another human. They're not birdprints, but whatever they are, they could have only come by air."

Emmeur looked slowly from side to side. "Aaagghh," he murmured, "we are so far from anywhere. Only something with wings and an extraordinary sense of smell could have found this place."

"What do you think they were?" said The Fool.

"The only creatures I think it could be," the Bird said slowly, "are Drocabodaws."

The Fool, shivering, took a deep breath.

"Droca what?" said Stormy, shivering now as well. She was glad of the thick coats that The Witch and Glamour had insisted they wear.

"Drocabodaw," repeated The Fool. "The flying lizard. Well—part lizard, part bird."

"But they're not real! They're just a story ... I ..." Stormy stopped. She remembered how many stories she had found turned out to be real.

"Braggardio!" muttered The Fool, pulling off his three-peaked hat and tearing at his thinning hair in his distraction. "It begins to fall into place."

"What are you talking about?" said Stormy frantically. "Where's my dad?"

"But why point a finger at the Prince, Fool?" quizzed the Bird.

"I spent some moons in Oosaria in summers gone by. It wasn't commonknowledge—though such knowledge has a habit of becoming common to me—but in his youth, Prince Braggardio had a certain proclivity for cruelty toward creatures. It would not surprise me if he had found a way of ensluicing the Drocabodaw."

"If it is true, the picture looks grim," said The Gricklegrack.

"Aye," agreed The Fool. "And I'll bet my big toe Braggardio and Prince Toromos will be at the helm of one of the warships making up the Lumbiana River."

"Well, the knowledge of their rough position will aid us somewhat in our journey to find your father. It is a fair guess they hold him captive on board one of those vessels."

"I'll kill him. I'll kill both of them," said Stormy, meaning Braggardio and Toromos. Seeing her determined face, The Fool was inclined to take her seriously. She showed no hysteria, only calm determination. "But how did they even know my dad was up north?" she said, intent.

She answered her own question.

"A spy," she said flatly. She remembered Sonia, picking up Waltherbald's message and putting it safely away, in the kitchen at Bald Mountain Castle, that day which seemed so long ago. It was a horrible thought. But Stormy had begun to grow up, and when you grow up, horrible thoughts cannot so easily be pushed away.

"Get back in the harness," the Black Bird said quietly.

"Wait!" Stormy walked a few paces towards something glittering in the snow that the other two had missed. She pulled at the silver thing.

"The wonderlook," said The Fool.

"Bring it," said the Bird. "We must head south. No time to rest. Except ..." He smiled, showing his great teeth as Stormy climbed up his feathered side. "Except rest your mind. And remember Stormy, your father is too precious to the Oosarians as a bargaining tool for them to do him any real harm—yet. I will tell you more later, for there is much more to tell. I will tell you things about your mother. I know you have been wanting to ask. But now I must rest my tongue and focus my eyes. We will be passing over northern villages forthwith, and I want no one to see us as we go."

Once more, Emmeur took off into the sky, shooting up from the ice ledge outside the cavern. As he soared upward, Stormy pressed her head against his warm, feathered sides and tried to rest her mind. But all she could think was they were going to war. For there is war even in sort-of fairy tales. This would be her first. But not, alas, her last.

Chapter 16
THE BELLS OF WAR

Back at Bald Mountain Castle, things were more frenzied with each new message bird from Rockport. In the last two days, as the Oosarian longship army progressed northwards up the western sea, the message birds came from closer and frantically closer to home.

After the departure of Nukeander and the Oosarians, and more updates from King Jude, Geraldo had put the Morainian defense program on full alert. Based on the reasonable premise that the defense of Morainia against outside aggressors was—spies and traitors excepted—in the interests of all Morainians, it was an organized program of mutual aid.

All who could help did. All who were willing, which meant almost everyone, and all who were able, which really meant everyone over the age of nine to even the oldest grandparents, were being mobilized. It was how Morainia pretty much functioned under the normal circumstances of daily living, and this was all the more heightened by the Oosarian threat.

Morainians were a peace loving people. But they didn't like being pushed around.

There were jobs for all abilities. Feeding those in frontline positions, cleaning and sharpening weapons, relieving troops and scouts on a shift basis. Most people over the age of fifteen had some experience of active patrol service, occasionally repelling spies in the foothills where the Bald River Falls cascaded into the Lumbiana.

On rare occasions there had been skirmishes along these frontlines. The few older men and women still living, who had been young when Jakerbald became King and Walterbald was a boy, remembered the last full-scale defense of the kingdom.

Gwynmerelda had trained in Morainian defense exercises, but never the real thing. She retrieved her armor from the storehouse the very morning that Stormy and The Fool had taken to the air with The Gricklegrack.

The armor lay on the bed now as she wiggled herself into deer hide breeches, which she would normally not be seen dead in. She pulled the hip straps tight, and picked up the breastplate. As she stood adjusting the straps there was a knock at the door.

"Enter."

"It's only me," said Geraldo. He came in, a smile chasing the wearylines across his faithful-comrade face. "You look—"

"I look like shit," the Queen groaned. She pulled her hair back and tied it behind her head. That made her look even less the glamorous Queen that Morainians knew her as. She did, however, look imposing.

Geraldo bowed. "I bring you something for the battle." From behind his back he presented a hatchet.

Gwynmerelda studied it. "It was hers, wasn't it?"

Geraldo nodded.

It was a light, sleek, hatchet, specifically designed to be wielded by a woman. There was no jewel-encrusted hilt, but the metalwork was of exceptional quality, and there was an inscription on the handle:

To Ursula, with all my heart. Walterbald. xx

"But this belongs to Stormy," protested Gwynmerelda.

"Stormy is with the Bird by now. There is no greater weapon than The Gricklegrack to protect the Princess. This hatchet is a queen's hatchet and you are the Queen."

Gwynmerelda fought back a tear and held still. And then the muscles in her cheeks quivered, as she relented and the tears came.

Geraldo half moved towards her, she towards him. It was awkward. She still had the hatchet in her hand. He was tentative, but they managed a hug of sorts. Geraldo felt the mountains of the breastplate digging uncomfortably into his chest, but the Queen hung on with all her might.

"Morainia has never given up before, dear Queen, and there is no reason that we should do so now."

"But some of us will die?"

"Probably. But we have no choice."

"I know," she winced. "I just can't bear the thought of it all."

Geraldo kissed Gwynmerelda on the forehead.

"You are a true queen," he said.

Before the Queen could reply there was a new knock on the door. Jakerbald and Gigi burst into the room.

"Bad news," said the former King, "from The Witch in the

Ditch. And this—." He gave some small pieces of paper to Geraldo.

"It's Walterbald," said Gigi. "He's been kingnapped from the northlands."

Gwynmerelda said nothing. She gave a faint shudder and pulled herself up to her full height, as if to meet whatever came.

"It seems that the Oosarians have some flying creatures in their employ. They took Walterbald this morning," said Jakerbald.

"And that's not the worst of it," said Geraldo, looking up momentarily from the paper he held in his hand. "This is the Oosarian ransom note."

> We, the Oosarian fleet, will be anchored by Bald River Falls before dawn tomorrow. You are probably aware by now we hold your King Walterbald prisoner, and will not release him until the battle force of the Oosarian guard have been granted safe passage up the Falls Road. Any sign of aggression will seal Walterbald's death.
>
> signed, Your humble conqueror, Prince Toromos, servant of Queen Nukeander of Oosaria. Lion of the South.

"They're bluffing," assured Jakerbald.

"Maybe," said Geraldo.

"Anything else?" asked the Queen, straightening her back and chasing the worrylines away with a look of determination.

"Yes," said Jakerbald. "Rogerley Bishop and his clique are gone. The kitchen girl Sonia betrayed us. They plotted Walterbald's kingnapping, and the Oosarian battle fleet sailed north as we were sitting down to dinner with Nukeander."

"To Eagle Cave then, comrades," said Gwynmerelda, standing up, clutching the axe she still held. "And we'll see what schemagems we can make to throw at *them*."

Chapter 17
TRANSKINKERY AND THE CHICKEN MAGICIAN

By early evening The Gricklegrack and his passengers were nearing the northwestern fringes of the wider Morainian kingdom. As the Bird had suggested, they came back to earth for shelter and sustenance in the forest before nightfall.

The Bird disappeared for what seemed a short while, and came back with a redfish, maybe three feet long.

"Shall I do the honors?" asked The Fool. Taking a knife from his belt, he slit the belly of the fish and began gutting it.

"I took the liberty of eating," said the Bird. "You'll have to eat yours raw of course. Your human predilection for cooked food? We can't afford ..."

"... the smoke signals," finished The Fool. "No problem," and he looked to Stormy.

"I know, I know," said Stormy, "good brain food." The Fool handed her a piece of the pink-red flesh. She winced as she took a bite, but it tasted far better than she'd thought.

Then the questions began again. Brain food indeed. The Gricklegrack had told her many things as they flew, with her ear pressed to his feathered side. But she had a lot more things she wanted to know now. "You said my dad had a theory that intelligent life existed before the dark times. I don't understand how all the stories could be wrong, how everything I learned at school, all the books in the library could be wrong."

The Gricklegrack preened his feathers and considered how to answer.

"They're not all wrong. But there are other stories than the ones you know. We grickles have a whole library's worth of our own. Then new discoveries change what we thought we knew. Twenty winters ago everyone to a man would swear that water could not run uphill. But your father invented a machine that made water run uphill. The story changes in good ways and bad ways. Ask The Fool here. A master of stories. The story changes as it gets passed along."

The Fool was busy chewing on a hunk of fish, and he grinned with his mouth full. Stormy wanted to ask the Bird if he and his kind had a completely different beginning story to the one she had been taught, but Emmeur was on a roll now. Even The Fool could not get a word in.

"Take your own story. We, your father and I, got the message from Gwynmerelda. You accidentally killed a prince in self defense, but already, in a couple of days, the chittle-chattle tells how you brutally murdered him while he slept."

"Did not. I—. It was an *accident.*"

"I know that, and you know that, but the story itself does not know that. The story adapts to what its listeners want to hear. You pass the story down across tens of winters, and it travels across land and sea where beings have different languages, and before you know, it's a tale of how the brave princess, disguised as a boy-jester, made it her business to travel the west, ridding

117

the land of corrupt princes."

"But I don't want that. I don't want to kill princes. I hate the story."

"Ah yes, but the story has a life of its own now. However some things remain more or less intact. The essence of the story, which in this case is the unusual fact that the Princess kills the prince, is, well, in fact ... 'er, a fact."

"He was the one who came prowling and groppelling into my bedroom," Stormy protested.

"Yes exactly!" the Bird agreed. "The devanimal is in the details, but the real details remain invisible to everyone else," said the Bird. "So when the story gets out into the world, the people hearing it, the audience, re-imagine the invisible details to make the story fit their situation or their way of thinking. They make it their own."

"But they can't!" said Stormy stormily.

"But they do," said The Fool. "We all do. It's the way we are."

"After hundreds of winters," the Bird went on, "there is no telling how different a story is from the way it was first told. We wouldn't even know if the story was based on real happenings, or just grew out of a pretendsuppose night tale."

The Fool nodded vigorously in agreement as he chewed more of the fish.

"Now, leapfrog for a moment. Think of the passage of hundreds and thousands of winters. Your father has a theory that creatures, flowers, and trees are like stories. We all possess a fundamental essence made up of invisible details, or kinks as

Walterbald calls them. Then as the forces of nature change—
the earth belches and spews lava, the sea rises and falls, the ice
advances or retreats—these kinks change, too, and shape what
creatures and plants look like. What we look like."

"Over millennia, those invisible kinks made you a girl, and
me a bird. However, if we went far enough back, you and I
might once have been fish." In this, The Gricklegrack was closer
to the truth than he knew. The Fool paused, then shrugged and
took another piece of the redfish.

"Nooo!" said Stormy as she saw dream pictures of strange
creatures in her head. "That really is devanimaltalk."

"The way your father describes it, we creatures become
transkinked, according to how our invisible details respond to
nature. It's a leap of imagination, but we have been uncovering
facts that seem to back it up. You see the process speeded up in
how your actual experience has become transfigured into the
folk tale of The Three Dead Princes."

"What? What?" Stormy could not believe what she was
hearing. It seemed that, whether she liked it or not, she had
been cast as the prince-killer extraordinaire. The play had been
written, and they were already performing it in the streets. It
was not a good feeling.

"For instance. Your mother grew roses," said the Bird. And
suddenly Stormy was rapt with attention again. "She spliced
red and lilac roses, and cross-bred them and cross-bred them
again, until eventually she grew a deep purple rose that had
never before been seen."

Stormy had seen that rose growing in the gardens at Bald

Mountain Castle. The story people told was that Ursula had been able to grow a purple rose, because of the enchantment that she felt for Waltherbald, and he for her.

"Ursula was as clever as she was beautiful. She saw qualities in each rose, for each individual rose is different, as each person or bird differs from his kin. Over successive growing seasons she brought out certain kinks that enabled her to make a new rose."

"Your grandfather is a chicken magician," piped up The Fool, finally finished with his fish and wiping his mouth with the back of his hand. "The Mountain White, which gives us eggs in winter. Most chickens don't lay when it is cold like the Morainian cold. But Jakerbald is a great cross-breeder. A hardier chicken than that the world has never seen."

"It was Ursula's rose growing and Jakerbald's chickens that led Walterbald to his theory," said Emmeur, "that all living things can be and have been transfigured by nature. That a certain rogue quality can become stronger in a creature down through generations. And if it is useful in how that creature deals with the changed nature of the world, it becomes part of that creature's essence. If the earth were old enough, the creature could be changefigured again and again over hundreds and thousands of winters. It happens so slowly we never see it happening before us—unless we are growing roses or raising chickens.

"Sometimes a new creature emerges, and maybe meets up with the old one, and they are two different creatures. Gricklegrack lore tells of many different creatures on the eastern side of the Mezzala Ice Mountains. Like people, like birds, but different in some way. Perhaps whoever, or whatever is on Nukeander's longships are transkinked humans?"

"Or, maybe, we are transkinked from them," offered The Fool.

"But how can the world be so old? My wangodmatist teachers say it is sixty-two hundred summers old," insisted Stormy.

"The dark times happened. Whatever caused them, whoever was around before, during or after, godmatists and scientics alike agree, that they happened. I have seen the evidence with my own eyes. Far to the north a whole mountainside collapsed after an earthrumble. There are thousands of winters of white ice lying over what seems like a thin strip of black ice, which could be a few hundred winters thick. Below the black ice are thousands upon thousands of winters more of deeper gray-white ice. One can read it, like the rings in a tree. It was bogglingly too many layers to count.

"You humans tell tales of the Black Cat and his mountains."

"You've seen the Black Cat?" quivered Stormy, suddenly remembering the talking cat from her dream.

"Yes. But an old proverb says that you will not find the Black Cat because ..."

"... because he found the sun and changed his coat," sang Stormy, finishing the line.

"I have seen the Black Cat. He was frozen dead in the Great Ice Wall. That does not mean he no longer exists. However, my fellow grickles and I have travelled the northlands for generations. We know of many strange beasts, but no black cat bigger than a castle cat. But—," and here The Gricklegrack paused for effect, "… I have seen the White Cat. He is indeed a giant among beasts. I did not stick around long enough to see if he talked."

"Could it have been an albino?" spouted The Fool. "Like the white man who sells white rabbits in the marketplaces of the south. Like a juggler I once knew. White with pink eyes."

"No. There were a whole family of them, almost invisible against the snow. I saw their red eyes coming just as I took to the air. Just in time. A moment before I smelled them—two moments after, they would have been upon me. It may be that, like the snowfoot hare, the black cat changed his coat for winter, and now because he lives on the fringes of the Ice Wall, he stayed white."

"But you are black. You live up north. Why aren't you the great white bird?" protested Stormy.

"Why aren't I black and white, like the snow-capped eagle, or the magpie, or the white-walled dolphin? Most Morainians are fair skinned. Your mother, though not originally from Morainia, was fair skinned, like most northern peoples. But you, Stormy, have darker skin than either your father or your mother. Yet you look like both of them. Somewhere in your story, your mother's father, or his mother's mother, or someone along one of the lines, travelled from across the world. And part of the traveler is in you."

Stormy was boggled by such wild thoughts. But as they came

from The Gricklegrack, and were sprinkled with remembrances of her mother, she also felt strangely comforted.

"It is a mystery," The Bird continued. "It may be that the wangodmatists are right, that the creator came and put man on the earth to teach the animals a lesson. If that were the case, however, then I would not be talking to you now. I have read the wangodmatist *Book of Life* and there is no talking bird in any of its myriad tales, before, during, or after the dark times. The problem is that some wangodmatists believe, or pretend to believe—it really doesn't matter which—that their story is rigid as a metal pole. Worse, given the chance, they would use their book as a weapon to beat your father around the head with."

Stormy winced, and the Fool gingerly put a reassuring arm around her shoulder.

"Tools over weapons, my dear girl," said the Bird. "Ideas over ideologies. Like the wonderlook. It helps us see things in new ways. If we have the tools and the imagination to look at the world afresh, then we will never cease to be startled by what we find in it."

Through a break in the trees, Stormy saw the first night star far above, and remembered that she had flown here. After everything that had happened—was still happening before her very eyes—she wondered, *how can the world ever look the same again?*

Chapter 18
TWO DEAD PRINCES

The Lumbiana River was mighty and wide, even in darkness. Prince Toromos stood on deck as he often did, stroking his prized gold cannon, congratulating himself on the subterfuge by which he had come to possess it. He loved that cannon. His chest swelled with pride as he marveled at the Oosarian miracle. He called it the Oosarian miracle. His brother called it the Oosarian miracle. His mother called it the Oosarian miracle.

A shadow moved at Toromos's side and a ghostly white face appeared in the moonlight. It was Queen Nukeander, dressed in mourning black. "The time will soon be with us, son," she rasped, putting a bony hand on the prince's shoulder. "Not only shall we take Morainia, but we will avenge the death of your brother in triplicate."

They had repeated this mantra, in various forms, since Nukeander's cortege had rendezvoused with the procession by Bridgeton on the Lumbiana. They had convinced themselves that the ships—and the cannon were bigger than anything this corner of the sort-of-fairy tale world had ever seen. To look at Prince Toromos strutting about the bridge of the lead vessel like a puffed up peacock for his mama, one would think the technology was all Oosarian. This was not the case.

Two summers previously, much smaller, clumsier Oosarian warships had encountered bizarre never-before-seen vessels in the waters by the furthest southern isles. Those ships were strange, and those who sailed in them stranger still. They were sort-of-men. They were like men, and then they were not like men. They walked upright. They talked. They had more hair than Oosarian men, and a much more pronounced brow. They had very good night vision and great strength. And melding the ocean-going technologies of the strange men with their own, the Oosarians had built these longships and stolen the idea for the cannon. Using the strange men as muscle power had enabled the Oosarians to drop anchor in view of Bald Mountain, on this dark night before the dawn.

More than anything, the sort-of-men laughed. They laughed when they woke up. They laughed as the afternoon wind caught the sails and eased their passage up the Lumbiana. They laughed even more as they rowed the great ships at the end of the day against the meandering Lumbiana current, and against the katabatic night wind. They were always laughing.

When they heard that they were invading Morainia, with the hastily added *casus belli* of avenging the murder of Mercurio, they laughed hardest of all.

Toromos had only shed droca tears for his younger brother's death, for he knew all his brothers to be rivals.

"Wangod bless you with a conqueror's dreams," hissed the Black Queen as she bade him good night.

Prince Toromos turned to watch Nukeander go, and as the shadows swallowed her up, he heard that incessant laughing once again. He smiled, for he cared little now that the giggling slaves had brought him to the brink of his destiny. He sang to himself,

Tomorrow Tomorrow,
Tomorrow is an ugly day,
For any who stand in my way.

Down below in the hold, King Walterbald of Morainia defied his own thoughts by quite enjoying some gruel his captors had provided for his evening meal.

As a king, Walterbald was worried, of course. He knew how formidable a force was about to assault Morainia. But as a scientic and an explorer, he couldn't help but be fascinated by what he had seen on the Oosarian vessel. From where, he wondered, had the sort-of men come? The laughing soldiers of the south were like no life-form Walterbald had ever seen. Who was transkinked from who, he wondered now? These were surely very close relatives of humans. His sciential mind boggled. What force of nature had given them different tools than the western peoples? What exactly were those tools? The golden piece of pipe that graced the prow of Toromos's ship— the cannon they called it. What was that?

Most of all, he wondered, why would the sort-of men subject themselves to the Oosarians? How could the Oosarians possibly exert power over soldiers who, when they relaxed from their rowing, looked so carefree and strong?

There was something not quite right about it all. And

strangely, there was something about those southern sort-of men that gave Walterbald hope. It wasn't a rational hope, but as many a scientic had discovered before him, sometimes the things that weren't rational were the most rational of all.

Given the circumstances, Princess Stormy was having a fine Accidental Adventure. She would not have admitted this to others, and she found it hard to admit it to herself, but it was true.

The flight over the Twin Moraine Mountains, around the town of Morainia, and then along the loominated ribbon of the Bald River, was itself relatively short. As Emmeur had warned his passengers, they would initially by-pass Bald River Falls, staying north to join the Lumbiana downstream. Then by doubling back on themselves, dropping low over the forest on the north bank of the great river, they could steal a peek at the war fleet.

Stormy's heart leapt when she saw the twinkling lights of her hometown. It was not too much to say she was enjoying herself, even though her country's situation was dire. Stormy was not the first person to discover that having something difficult to do was exciting and frightening, both at the same time.

She could see nothing untoward in the darkness of the valley floor, out to where the Bald River cascaded in a spectacular waterfall into the Lumbiana below. That said, the Princess knew the Morainian Defense Guard would be fully deployed and ready. She thought of Gwynmerelda and wondered if she was there too. To her surprise, she found that she longed to see her stepmother.

As The Gricklegrack began to drop low, Stormy could smell the fir and pine trees she knew so well. The air was warmer here, and it was alive with the summer buzzing of life. Bats flitted zizzerhither, tracking down skeeters. She heard a long-eared owl somewhere below, and then she saw the glint of the moon on the Lumbiana.

"Geez-ar-us!" whispered The Fool.

The Gricklegrack looked round as if to command silence, and Stormy saw the luminescence of his blood-red eye rings.

Below them was the line of ships, anchored in a giant eddy of flat waters, a safe distance from the mighty Bald River Falls. With the quartermoon high in the sky and the Lumbiana chasing it into the eastern distance, the war fleet was silhouetted like a pack of dark, slumbering night monsters, speckled with the firefly eyes of kero-lamps.

There were ten ships, for Stormy counted them. They seemed only to promise heartache and misery to a girl who had only seen ships a quarter their size. Her heart sank, and she buried her head into the feathers of Emmeur's neck.

Only the Bird seemed unperturbed. "It could be worse," he mused.

"How could it be worse?" quizzed The Fool.

"If the longships had wings it would be worse," said the Bird.

And then it did get worse. From the prow of the lead ship there was a loud bang, and a fireball zipped across the whole width of the Lumbiana, smashing into the cliff opposite, and sending rocks tumbling. Toromos, in his eagerness for the morning to come, could not resist unleashing a cannon ball for the pure hell of it.

The Gricklegrack banked steeply to the left and climbed, hefting his mighty wings with a whoosh-shoosh of air.

The Fool groaned.

"What was that?" said Stormy, struggling for words, for no Morainian had ever witnessed anything resembling the explosive power of gunpowder.

"That, I believe," said The Gricklegrack "is precisely the kind of thing your father searches for. Magic, or more accurately mechanagics, that predate the western peoples."

Stormy looked back, but the great ships were only tiny black specks now. From this distance she could have picked them up and scrunched them between her fingers. She felt the balmy flush of the summer night again, as they crested the Falls and entered the hanging valley of the Bald River proper.

Before she knew it they were on the ground again. Voices surrounded them. In the dark, hands were helping her from the riding harness. Somebody murmured "Princess," and helped her to the ground. She wobbled as her feet searched for stability on the familiar but rough terrain. Then, an even more familiar voice reached into her heart.

"Alexandra!"

Stormy turned and threw herself the few short paces into Gwynmerelda's arms. Stormy buried her face in the familiar smell of the queen's hair where it fell from her helmet upon her shoulder.

"Come come, my darling. Come inside," whispered the Queen.

The Fool was being hugged by Jakerbald, and Geraldo ushered everyone in with the promise of hot food and drink. Gwynmerelda guided Stormy into the homely surroundings of Eagle Cave.

If any eagles had ever lived in this cave, it had not been in recent living memory. For this cave, which was close to Bald River Falls, but hidden by the out-crop from anyone coming up the Falls Road, had been the nerve center of Morainian defense activity for generations.

As Stormy sat sipping soup, she looked again at the ancient pictures of eagle-like birds on the walls. Stormy had first seen these pictures when her father showed them to her as a younger child. Now she saw how one bird stood like a giant next to the human stick figures in its path.

She saw and remembered the bird's ochre red eyes, pigmented in part from the metals that lay beneath Morainia's mountainsides. She turned and saw The Gricklegrack, Emmeur, not twenty feet away in deep conversation with Geraldo, Gwynmerelda, The Fool, Jakerbald and some others she knew were battalion leaders of the defense force.

Along with a network of caves, mostly smaller than the one they were now ensconced in, the Morainian defenses involved an extensive series of buried earth lodges. Each housed twenty people or more, mostly scattered around the fringes of the forest where the valley sides began to rise away from the river, all the way back to the bottleneck of Bald River Gorge. The long meandering road that wound its way down from the Gorge was securely barricaded at the top of the Falls Road, along the northern bank of the river. From there, the road switched back and forth over a short mile to the northern bank of the Lumbiana, and the waiting war party.

The Princess put her empty soup bowl down and stood up.

"More soup love?" It was Grandma Gigi. She was joined by Grandma Wilson. "I can make you some goodnight tea," said Zilpher.

"No thanks," said Stormy. "I have to know what is happening," and she walked over to the other side of the cave.

There, gathered like an amateur football team—two goals down at halftime to the western champions—representatives from the various arms of the Morainian Defense Guard had gathered in an impromptu circle. A multifarious bunch of parents, grandparents, and lateens, who doubled in waking life as farmers, builders, foresters, and bakers. There was the man from the ditch committee, Fred's mother Claire, the message-bird mistress, and Athiane, who ran the library where Stormy worked ... now all taking on third jobs as war tacticians.

Stormy found a space for herself next to Fred. Fred smiled at her and he shuftied over to give the Princess more room.

Geraldo was chairing the meeting. "What say you, Captain Arahab?" he asked of one of the defense guards, who Stormy knew in ordinary Morainian life as an organizer of the farmers market.

"I wish we could hit them in the dark. We might stand a

chance then," Arahab said, looking at Stormy, "but me and the other captains. We all agree." There were murmurs of general assent from behind him. "We won't launch an all-out assault if they still have Walterbald. Though it be dangerous if we have to let the Uosarians march up the Falls Road. Very dangerous."

"How do we deal with the fireball thrower? asked Athiane,

"It's the slave army still worries me," Geraldo said.

"And what about the flying lizards?" asked The Fool.

Everyone was quiet for a moment. The Morainians are a pragmatic people, and they don't waste much energy on things they can't control. They tend to focus on what's in front of them, which is probably why they've lasted and thrived in this sort-of fairy tale world.

The flying lizards and fireballs could wait for now.

"Anyone know anything about Prince Toromos? What he's like as a commander?" asked Arahab.

"Toromos is vain and cruel, but he's not stupid. Braggardio was always the crazy one," Gwynmerelda said.

"I too have met Toromos," said The Fool, "and more recently than the Queen. He remains vain, but he is clever. He is a good tactician, but something tells me he is also a mite blind. I am guessing he thinks this huge technological leap in ocean power will scarify us into submission."

Stormy made an impatient gesture. After the Accidental Adventure of the last few days, she felt she'd earned the right to say her piece now. "Do we have a plan?" she said briskly to the Bird.

Surprised, Gwynmerelda looked at her. And the Queen, in

spite of her many worries, smiled.

Emmeur smiled too, though he hid it when Stormy looked a demand his way.

"I—, we, The Fool and I, have a sort-of-plan," he said.

"Oh," said Stormy. "Will it sort-of-work?"

"I am sort-of-hoping so."

"And so what is it, Gentelmengracks?" asked the Princess. At this, all three of her grandparents smiled. She looked just like her father in that moment.

"Fighting ships are all very well so long as one is not attacked from the air. It's like the redfish you ate for dinner. He never saw me coming."

The council considered this.

"It is a gross act of war, there being ten warships below the falls," said Jakerbald finally. "Us being able to inflict a blow against them is the very last thing they expect. You're right. If we can unsettle them in some way, then it will not be as one-sided as they might have thought."

"This golden tube that sends fireballs. You'll aim for that," said Geraldo, sensing where they were going with this.

"Yes," said The Gricklegrack. "Only, I can't do it alone." He rubbed at his feathers and looked up at the ceiling of the cave. "I need someone—one person—to balance with the rock, and to tell me when to let it fly." He cleared his throat. "It should be a smallish person. One who has already proved she … I mean she or he … has rapport with me in the air."

Well, of course Stormy knew who he meant. She looked at the faces of those gathered around her, and then at her feet, looking for the strength to make the decision for herself. She did not like it one bit. She looked at Emmeur, and thought she saw a look of reassurance.

After a heartbeat of hesitation the Princess announced, "I'm doing it then."

"No, you are not!" screeched the Queen.

"Am too. Emmeur says he needs me to do it."

"Aggh Mmmm!" intoned The Gricklegrack. "It's true, gracious Queen."

"That's settled then," said Stormy. She said this in the determined way of a Princess who knows where her duty lies.

And the Queen, who was, as we have seen, as wise as she was beautiful, knew that it was so.

It was some time after midnight but a longer time before dawn, when Stormy was once again strapped to Emmeur's back.

They were only about a half-mile from the cave to the point where the Bald River cascaded off into the dark night below. Once down near the riverbank, Emmeur broke into a sort of jog. He remained very sure-footed, despite his size and the uncertain nature of the rocky terrain. Stormy felt the cool air skimming her cheeks.

The moon had passed its zenith and was moving towards the western sky now. As they neared the edge of the falls, The Gricklegrack slowed to a walk and then stopped. Stormy stared over the edge to the Lumbiana far below. The Bird sat down by the riverbank and sort-of-wiggled his whole rear end.

The noise of the water crashing below the cliff was

deafening.

He had given her instructions. When they took flight towards the ships, she was to wait for him to cry out. He had told her the flight would be very quick and warned her that his caaw would be deafeningly loud. As soon as she heard it, she was to tug with all her might at the feathers around the left side of his head where his chin would be, if he had one. He had her practice again now, finding the right spot with her fingers, taking hold of the feathers, but not pulling just yet. She felt that she knew what she had to do, but she was still puzzled. Where was the weapon? Unless, yes, of course, Emmeur had secreted it in his undercarriage.

Emmeur turned his head half towards her and winked with a fearsome red eye. He stood and exchanged the weight from foot to foot, and Stormy guessed correctly that the time was now. She braced herself. But then, all at once, a thought hit her over the head.

Her dad. Where was her dad? Was he on the lead ship? How could she have forgotten?

"Wait!" she cried out.

But it was too late. The Gricklegrack took a short run, then pushed off from the last remaining ground. They plummeted downwards. Stormy's stomach dropped. She shrieked but no noise came out of her mouth.

She hoped against hope. With her eyes tightly slammed shut she concentrated all her energies into her outstretched left arm. Her fingers reached around the left side of Emmeur's neck in a claw shape.

They plunged headlong towards the ships, and Stormy, opening her eyes, saw the glitter of the gold cannon in the prow of the leader. What if it was that ship that held her dad? Emmeur opened his mouth, but before his cry could be heard, in her fear for her father, Stormy tugged with all her might.

Feather fragments came away in her hand as Emmeur's flight path bottomed out into a swooping curve. The spasmering of nerves from The Gricklegrack's neck enabled his undercarriage muscles to relax for the half-moment necessary.

The boulderous rock therein—big as a sheep—was ejected forthwith. And the moment after that, a scream rang out, but was almost immediately eclipsed by a loud splinterendering *kerrcrack*, as the rock smashed into the tip of the ship's prow below.

Stormy opened her eyes and saw they had missed the cannon. The boulder fell too soon, and had landed right at the tip of the prow. The Gricklegrack relieved of his heavy burden began to climb once more.

We missed the cannon. We were supposed to hit the cannon. It's my fault.

Freed of the weight of the rock, the Bird was suddenly much more airgile. He gave a raven about-turn—and for a moment The Gricklegrack was upside down with Stormy beneath him. Then they banked and sped back down toward the front line of ships to inspect the damage.

Emmeur dipped low, and Stormy could hear the whistling arrows. With a *kerthwack*, an arrow skidded off one of the restraining straps of her harness. She half-scrunched up her eyes

137

to shield them from the rushing air, but in the instant before the Bird veered abruptly up and away, she saw the body.

Well, she saw the boulder crushing the planks of the ship's deck. And she saw a pair of arms and legs out from under it. It wasn't likely that meant anything else.

"We weren't supposed to hit anybody!" she thought. "It's my fault."

She pressed her head against the Bird's neck and heard him say, "An accident. But perhaps a fortunate one."

And they began to soar away from the ships again, toward the Falls.

Stormy craned around to look into Emmeur's eye. From her position she could only see a scimitar flash of red iris. Had they been on the ground, she could not look him in the eyes as she could another person. She wouldn't be able to read the secrets of eyes that had been engineered tens upon tens of thousands of winters ago, for just such a *mission* as the one they had almost completed.

A grinding, guttural alarm *caww* of the Bird cut through to shake Stormy from the trance. Instinct forced her head around, and she saw not one, but two flying shadows pursuing them.

"The Drocas!" she screamed, her yell swallowed by the noise of the Falls, her stomach lurching.

Emmeur surged into a climb before the wall of water. They were now only feet away from the crashing falls, and Stormy shook herself as the spray lashed her face. Then the Great Bird arced around and away from the Falls to face their pursuers.

The Drocobadaws were as long as The Gricklegrack was tall, but they were much leaner. As The Fool had said, they were lizard-like, though it was hard to see any detail through the mist except their silhouette outlines.

Emmeur thought about trying to outfly the creatures, but he had been flying all day and had just hauled a weight that was really too heavy for him. He thought about the danger to his precious passenger. But the part of him that was raptor and predator knew the only choice was to fight.

As the flying gatoriles closed, Stormy saw the nearer one open its long ferociously beteethed snout, and *gack* some signal to its companion. She felt herself being wrenched, upside down

and around, as Emmeur suddenly flipped full circle and turned again.

Stormy saw the Great Bird snap its huge beak, the moonlight reflecting momentarily off its rows of razor teeth, and heard a crunching sound as they closed on the Drocobadaw's tail.

The Gricklegrack shook its head vigorously from side to side. Stormy reeled convulsively, but remained firmly strapped in. The lizard's tail had been severed off completely, sending its former owner spinning out of control into the darkness below.

Next Stormy heard a whooshing sound, and the ear splitting caw of The Gricklegrack, as the other Droca's tail spikes slammed into Emmeur's side, not a foot away from where her own thigh lay.

The Black Bird wheeled in pain, but not before grabbing the Droca with an outstretched talon. The creature writhed and spat, as Emmeur brought his opposable thumb-claw to bear, slicing into the lizard's wing and rendering it useless for flight. The beast plummeted to the water below and disappeared with a silent splash.

"M! Are you all right? Are you all right?" Stormy called urgently. But Emmeur remained silent, and seemed to be putting all his energy into lifting them both back over the lip of the Bald River Falls to safety.

Landing on the bench before Eagle Cave, Emmeur finally allowed himself to speak.

"I take it by your energies that you are unharmed, girl, and for that I am ecstatic."

Stormy could see the blood streaming from Emmeur's side

as she unbuckled herself. "But, but, but," she protested, trying to plug the wound with her hands.

"I will live," the Bird said. "But I fear I will be of little use should it come to fighting in the morning. I can rest and recuperate in the cave. As should you."

In the next moments, Jakerbald and Geraldo attended the Bird, and Gwynmerelda pulled Stormy to her chest.

"One of those warships rests easy on the riverbed. A museum for when all this is over," said the Bird.

"They got off the ship before it sank," Jakerbald said. "We saw them in the boats."

Stormy recoiled: "But— I—we—We killed a man! ... in the prow of the boat."

"Hush," said Gwynmerelda. "Hush."

The Queen thought it best not to tell Stormy what she had seen, standing at the top of the Falls watching the battle through the wonderlook. She had seen Prince Toromos, of course, standing in the prow of the ship, fondling his gold cannon. Right before the boulder hit.

Two dead Princes, Gwynmerelda thought. Best not to tell Stormy that. Not yet. Even if the Princess was becoming an adult. As a mother, the Queen judged her stepdaughter to have had enough excitement for one day.

Chapter 19
THE BATTLE OF BALD RIVER FALLS

Dawn broke over Morainia, as inevitably as the Bald River cascaded down to the Lumbiana below. So the sun peeked its flaring red brim over the eastern horizon, and with it the Oosarian forces, in full battle dress, began marching up the switchbacks of the Falls Road.

Their force was immense, and the loss of one ship with one leader was only a temporary setback.

A Morainian squad of lateens, ensconced in the near impenetrable forest bordering the Falls Road, followed the invaders' progress. The lead eyes nearest to the Oosarians had sent her companion scout back with word, up to the next scout, and so on, so that the news would travel as fast as was humanly possible up the climb.

Stormy and Gwynmerelda had only just emerged from Eagle Cave when the first daylight news runner came back. It was Fred. He was panting and gasping for breath, trying to get his words out.

"What is it?" urged Geraldo.

"The King lives, sir!"

Stormy and Fred's eyes met momentarily, and then she looked away. The immediate sense of joy that spread in waves around the massing Morainian front lines was like a pebble hitting water ... But then as the ripples radiated outwards, it was as if a heavier stone of dread was tossed into the mix.

"The slave army?"

"They march free of chains and fully armed," said Fred.

"It is as we feared then," spat Jakerbald. "We are more in number, for we are all Morainia, but they have more fully-trained soldiers."

"It will not be long," said Geraldo, and then, even though he felt sick to his stomach, he managed to address those within earshot in a clear and steady voice: "The King lives. The enemy marches. We shall attempt to engage in negotiation with the Oosarians before any fighting. If there is no resolution, and if they insist upon marching towards the Gorge with the clear intention of traveling beyond it ... then we will have no choice but to repel them en route, by any means."

It will be soon, thought Stormy. She thought of her father. She thought of Emmeur tending his wounds in Eagle Cave. And she thought of how she wanted this all to be over.

Remember that Morainians had no regular means of measuring small increments of time, so what was indeed a short time, felt to many gathered in the Bald River Valley like the yawning chasm of eternity.

And then time arrived. Time for hope, aspiration, and fear to fuse with the fabric of reality, as the noise of marching boots on a gravel rock road could be heard above the noise of the Falls.

The barricade at the top of the Falls Road had been opened in anticipation of the Oosarians' arrival. And as the invaders marched through it now, the Morainians in forward positions got their first glimpses of the enemy.

A phalanx of about a hundred of the tallest men among the Oosarian Guard came first, brandishing unsheathed swords. While this was clearly meant to strike fear into the defending forces, Jakerbald could not help think that those soldiers with their heavy Oosarian metal swords would have mightily tired arms before any fighting even began.

Behind this front group came another tightly packed group, made up of row upon row of the slave-men—and some women it could now be seen—that the Morainians had been so dreading. Those who were close enough could see the slaves' haircr arms, exaggerated brows, and flaring nostrils. The slave-men seemed more hunched up in the way they marched, more awkward looking. It was these differences, coupled with the lack of knowledge of what they actually meant in terms of fighting skill, which made the sort-of-men appear the more fearsome.

More Oosarians came behind these, and then the command core. The command was protected by a row of guards at the front and sides.

Behind the Oosarian Prince's Guard, in a space of his own to emphasize his humiliation, was paraded the chained and bruised King of Morainia. And immediately behind Walterbald were Prince Braggardio and Queen Nukeander, with their personal guards. One of the guards occasionally made a jab at Walterbald with a long spear.

Rogerley Bishop and his clique came next, and on and on the body of troops seemed to stretch back down the road, alternating banks of Oosarian Guards with those of the southern fighters.

It was all clearly well planned for maximum impact.

As the front forces came into the valley bottom proper, they began fanning out to the sides and edging slowly forward, to allow more men to come in behind them.

Under Geraldo's instruction a similarly arranged, though much smaller, Morainian Guard and command core advanced slowly to meet them.

It was all very tentative. Few of those present had actually known serious warfare first hand. It was almost as if no one knew quite what to do, now that whole divisions of the respective armies were facing each other. The fact that there was a hostage involved clearly complicated matters.

"We request circle, and to see our King," said a lone voice in clear crisp tones. It was Jakerbald.

There were a few moments of ominous silence, before Braggardio replied, "Very well."

Most Morainians had never seen the Princes of Oosaria, but Gwynmerelda and The Fool exchanged uncomfortable looks as they scanned the ranks for the missing Toromos. Their suspicions about that Prince's unfortunate end were confirmed.

Then, as if by magic, or because they had all learned how to do it in sort-of kindergarten, the main negotiating parties of each command core formed a circle. There was some confusion on the Oosarian side, as two or three of the sort-of-men inserted themselves in among their masters.

Walterbald was motioned to stand to the right of Braggardio, with a guard to his other side. Nukeander, seething in black battle dress, stood to their right, with her own guards. Rogerley Bishop stood on Braggardio's left, edging out the Oosarian probber Elijareen.

On the Morainian side, Geraldo was sandwiched by Arahab and Athiane to his left, and Jakerbald to his right. Gwynmerelda stood to the kingfather's left, and Stormy was at the Queen's side.

"Any who wish to speak shall enter the circle, and none shall harm him," Geraldo announced.

"It shall be so," said Prince Braggardio, looking to his mother for approval, and then he walked across the few yards towards Stormy.

Gwynmerelda felt her hand tighten on her hatchet hilt. The Prince came forward another step and looked the Princess in the eye. "The famous Prince Killer strikes again. My brother Toromos lies crushed to death by the rock you and your pet raven dropped upon the great Oosarian fleet. It is my duty to slay you now." But he made no move to go for his sword.

Stormy felt as if the rock they had dropped the previous night had fallen on her, too. She hadn't meant to hurt anyone! Yet here she was. "Prince Killer," this crazy looking Prince had called her.

There was a muted *aagghhing* and *ohhnnooing* from the assembled Morainians, a communal sinking feeling as the fact of Toromos' death sunk in, and then silence.

Gwynmerelda looked at The Fool. She could tell he was thinking the same thing: With two brothers dead, Braggardio was the undisputed head of The Oosarian forces. They both knew that Braggardio was the most pyskotic and unpredictable of the bunch.

Geraldo took a step forward. "According to the customs of the western peoples we shall offer the necessary recompense for your loss."

"You would give me all of your precious metals?" laughed Braggardio, but his mirth was cut short by Queen Nukeander.

"We will take whatever recompense we desire, but we shall also re-write the laws of the west here and now, and exact a mother's revenge."

Braggardio, trying to step outside of his mother's shadow, turned theatrically and drew his sword. In brandishing the blade he deliberately flaunted the previous rules regarding this negotiating process. He walked around the inner space of the circle as if he already owned Morainia, clearly enjoying his moment. And then he strutted back over to his side of the circle and held the tip of his blade to Walterbald's bruised face. Still no Morainian made a move to reciprocate, even though their collective insides were straining and gurgling.

Turning to Stormy again the Prince laughed. "You will die here today, girl, but first you will see those you love perish."

"Yes," muttered Gwynmerelda. "Hysterical the little boy, becrazed the full grown man."

Stormy looked at Walterbald who remained impassive in the midst of his captors. Seeing her father a hostage, and looking into the hate-wells of Braggardio's eyes, did much to evaporate the remorse she had been feeling. Looking at Queen Nukeander extinguished every last drop. Finally she could stand it no more. Hardly knowing what she was doing, Stormy took a step forward.

"The Prince Killer wishes to speak," sang Braggardio, baiting and teasing.

And like something came to her from a dream, she announced, "I have tools."

Braggardio's perplexion was cut short by a rasping laugh.

"*Argghh! Arrgghh! Arrgghh!* Hear that brethsisteren?" a new and robust voice called out. "She has tools. She has the tools."

All turned in amazement to look at the source of this interjection. It came from the strange man who was stood closest to Prince Braggardio and Probber Bishop. The man, for he certainly was a kind of man, had shaken the look of deference that he and his kind had previously expressed towards the Oosarians. Quite suddenly this new sort-of-man seemed to stand taller and more imposingly than before.

"My brothers lie dead," Prince Braggardio said, outraged, "and we are supposed to listen to this gibbering half-man?" Bishop and the Oosarian coterie murmured assent, but were cut short by a deep guttural laugh. Even the Black Queen looked unnerved.

A deep guttural gigglanth laugh. "*Gha gha gah ha ha!*"

And now the creature's comrades—freed from the shackles that had held them as they had rowed the Oosarian ships north, were also freed from the pretence they had been keeping with the Oosarians. They stretched tall and began to laugh too. The Oosarian Guards now appeared not quite so formidable amidst their suddenly not-so-sort-of-slaves.

The laughing, the incessant laughing which had driven Braggardio half crazy on the voyage from Oosaria, was like no Morainian save King Walterbald had heard before. It now rang around the lip of the Bald River Valley. Then it ended abruptly, almost as soon as it had begun.

"The Prince is dead! Long live the Prince ... Killer! *Arrgghh Arrgghh Arrgghh*," shouted the sort-of-man, stepping into the circle, staring down Braggardio and then looking directly at Stormy. He laughed again.

If—as the many tacticians on both sides began pondering— the transkinked-men and women were now not with the Oosarians, then quite suddenly the Morainian warriors were no longer necessarily outnumbered.

Stormy was confused. Walterbald, against his better judgment felt his cracked lips break into a half smile. He quickly hid the expression, hoping none had seen it. Only Gwynmerelda had seen the flicker and, though her own face remained impassive, she felt her heart burst into a warm flame of hope.

"Allow me to introduce myself," said the laughing man.

"Silence! You insolent creature," bellowed Braggardio.

"Let the man speak!" yelled a voice from the crowd.

Unnerved, his mind racing desperately for a new plan, Braggardio bit his lip. Nukeander was about to speak but the laughing man cut her off.

"I am General Ghazali, and we," he said, arms aloft to indicate all his kinfolk, "are the free and noble knights of the Andean Kwestpeditionary Force. We travel from the roof of the world, which is also near the bottom of the world. Some call us men, some call us monkeys, but we are something else again. We are gigglanthropic by nature, and we are gigglanths in person." All the other gigglanths laughed appreciatively.

"Devanimaltalk!" fumed Rogerley Bishop. "These foul creatures are the blasfenemies of all good wangodfearing people," he shouted, trying to rouse some support among his fellow Morainians. There were some murmurs of confusion.

"Tiz beyond belief, Bishop!" spat Ghazali. "You would step over dead princes and ride on Andean backs to your glorious enthronement as puppet over Morainia, and yet you openly denounce us as lesser creatures. You want to eat your cake and not-shit-it, but I'll wager you'll do neither this day."

Bishop opened his mouth to speak, but then closed it rather than dig himself in deeper.

"You must not have heard my son," screamed Nukeander. "He said silence!"

"*Agh*, Queen Nukeander, Prince Braggardio. If you can contain your pumpeduppery for one second!"

Ghazali held the flat of his hand up, stressing to the Oosarians that they should remain quiet. "My comrades and I have been silent for you for long enough, quizzleprinks!" And he laughed.

"You call that unbearable laughing being silent?" spat Braggardio.

Ghazali laughed again, "*Arrggah! Arrggah! Arrggah!*" and then composing himself. "We have a saying where we come from. *You laugh … or you die!* So we laugh."

In this matter Ghazali was closer to the truth than he knew.

The giglanthropoid laugh did in fact emerge from kinks within, that tens of thousands of summers previously had emerged as a human adaptation to the choking black dust of the dark times.

Braggardio fumed some more.

"Take care not to, *arrggh, arrggh*, enrage my comrades with your insults, Prince. Or I will set the Prince Killer upon you!"

More laughter.

Braggardio obeyed despite himself.

"Shall I continue?" asked Ghazali of the immediate circle around him.

"Please do," said Walterbald courteously.

"Silence, prisoner!" the Black Queen clamored.

Braggardio elbowed Walterbald in the ribs. His panic was beginning to reveal itself.

Ignoring them, Ghazali raised his long arms as if he were about to conduct an orchestra.

"We Andeans are present here today to do no one's bidding." Then, giving Nukeander and Braggardio a particularly stern look, he added, "Other than our own."

The gigglanth then turned and focused his attention upon Stormy once more. He said very calmly, "My dear Princess. You were saying?"

Stormy had completely forgotten, if she ever knew, what she was supposed to be saying.

"The tools, girl?" Ghazali reminded her.

"Yes, yes, the tools …" And Stormy had neither the mistiest idea what had possessed her to announce the tools, less still what the tools were.

"Tool, tools, I live by the tools. And the tools—er."

"For nobadness sake, girl," said the General with a mild hint of impatience, "What are the tools of your trade?"

I don't have a trade, thought Stormy. But as she thought it, she happened to glance to her left and see The Fool. The Fool saw her look and he returned it, with the same slight nod of his head that he'd given her that night in the Grackle Tavern. She'd seen soldiers then, and she saw them now. She lifted her arms to the natural amphitheatre that the u-shaped Bald River valley provided, and then words came as if in answer to her dreams:

> *Fellow soldiers, stand at ease, hush-now, take rest,*
> *And I'll tell a tale to tickle you red.*
> *There's a prophecy, there's a quest, there's a Storm in the west*
> *But a war? Would be most ill advised!*

At this there was a slow, building hum of approval, mostly from the Andeans and the Morainians, but also it must be said, from some of the Oosarian foot soldiers. The louder derision came from those who were grouped around the Oosarian command and Bishop's cadre of wangodmatists.

> *"By the great God Joke it is She. And I Ghazali*
> *Am humbled in thy presence, Your Majesterley"*

And the General bowed to the Princess.

Stormy, returning the bow, continued:

153

Brave knights you are welcome, if you come in peace.
And we wish you safe passage to the—

Here Stormy faltered for a half breath. Looking around at the assembled masses for inspiration, she was aware of the strengthening warmth of the rising sun on her face. The same sun that the Black Cat had said would set her father free …

… And we wish gigglanths safe passage to the East."

The eastern passage through the Mezzala Mountains, which Stormy had seen from the air. How she did know in that moment, that this was of even the slightest importance to General Ghazali and the gigglanth people, Stormy had no idea until the day she died.

It was, though.

For the Andean beginning story, and their cultural history stretching back a couple of thousand winters, told of a fantastic otherworld, near the top of the world, east of the impassable mountains. According to *their* legend, it was where their ancestors had lived and built their great civilization. It was there that the Andeans would now find their destiny.

If this all seems very convoluted, that is because, like most origin myths, it was. Though certainly no more convoluted than the story of the Wangod and the animals. Like most prophetic stories, the Andean myth would be refined and rewritten over time, to accommodate changes that would otherwise have shaken the story to its core and shattered its believability.

For a story to survive, especially a prophetic one, someone has to periodically weed out the inconsistencies and retrospectively insert some anticipatory detail of what actually came to pass.

In this case, the great sleeping plague and the thousand-winter enslavement of the Andeans was in fact a virulent bout of Oosarian flu, followed by a practical decision to hitch their ride north by attaching themselves to the Oosarians. The symbiotic relationship between the Oosarians and the Andeans had produced the fleet of warships that now sat—minus one—in the Lumbiana River. Thus from the Andean point of view, the enslavement was more a round of seasons' construction contract than a millennial straightjacket. The match of prophecy and fact was hazy, but it was good enough for Ghazali and his comrades. It was for somebody else to hone the details later.

Ghazali and his comrades saw in Princess Stormy a warrior girl who sort-of-fit-the-bill of their legendary redeemer, who would point them in the right direction east. Thus in the moment immediately following Stormy's uttering the word "east," the whole valley seemed to erupt with cacophonic laughing and chanting.

General Ghazali lifted his arms once more in a gesture bidding silence, and approached the Princess.

"Dear Princess."

"Stormy," said Stormy.

"Ah, Stormy. Yes of course." He held out a hand to shake, and as she took it, and he knelt before her. "Stormy. Great Princess, Great Prince Killer! Most Royal Highlariness! Your

Majesterly. I am honored beyond Time to behold the living brownskin girl of ancient Andean prophecy."

He laughed, for as we are now keenly aware, gigglanths were always laughing, whether or not it was an opportune moment or not. "We, the mighty Andean Kwestpediter knights, hereby pledge to do you and your people no harm. All we ask is you grant us safe passage through your kingdom."

Stormy did not know what to think or where to look, so she looked into Ghazali's eyes. "I, 'er ... Granted!" she said, then glanced quickly to Walterbald for reassurance. The King nodded and smiled back at his daughter proudly.

Stormy opened her mouth as if to say something and then exhaled. She looked to her father and he nodded again.

"Tell us more," she said to Ghazali.

"I will," said Ghazali, "but first off methinks we must resolve this standoff," indicating with his long arms the variously arrayed forces of Morainians, Gigglanths, Oosarians, and the odd few other stragglers.

The general cupped his hands around his mouth and spoke in a megaphone voice. It was nowhere near as loud as The Gricklegrack's cry, but very loud for a man projecting his voice unaided.

"All those in favor of war say aye!"

There were a few limp ayes, mostly from those Oosarians who felt themselves in range of the watchful eyes of Queen Nukeander and Prince Braggardio. The loudest voices were Braggardio himself and Rogerley Bishop.

"Noted," said Ghazali. "All those against, say aye." And

the full chorus of the hundreds upon hundreds gathered in the Bald River Valley erupted in unison. Some even threw their hats into the air, and everywhere she looked Stormy saw people and gigglanths cheering, hugging whoever was closest to them.

When the ruckum had died down some, a snake-like voice shrieked: "Not so fast!" It was Rogerley Bishop, jockeying for position in the confusion of the morning's events. Turning first to the Queen of Morainia and then to Walterbald, the probber pointed a finger at Gwynmerelda:

"You think this harlot fit to be your Queen? Oh yes, intrepid King. For while you have been away on your scientical, blasfemical travels, you have been cuckolded by your wife and this man." Bishop twirled around on the spot to point at Geraldo.

"My spies—" Bishop began.

"Yes, your spies," snarled Gwynmerelda, "not only almost cost Walterbald his life, but also betrayed the whole of Morainia."

The Queen waved her hatchet, the Queen's hatchet, and winking at Geraldo, made a gracefully darting movement towards the probber.

"You blithering idiot," she spat at Bishop thwacking him hard on his rumpside with the flat of the axe. "Even the schoolchilder know that Geraldo finds his comfort in being flameringly man-to-man."

More raucous laughter, from Andeans and Morainians alike. Bishop was left spluttering and gibbering, but no words came out of his perfidious mouth. Queen Nukeander glared like the image of death.

In the pregnant pause that followed, Braggardio snapped out of his trance, the pyskosicks flaring new life into his eyes. His moment was escaping him and he badly wanted it back.

"You forget, so I shall remind you all," he barked, commanding silence. "This whorlet cessprince killed my brothers. It remains my right and my duty to challenge you …" He turned on Stormy weighing his sword. "A fight, Prince Killer? To the death!"

Chapter 20
THREE DEAD PRINCES

"Never!" came the shout. A teenage boy rushed forward. "I'll fight thee in her place."

It was Fred. Poor Fred.

Walterbald moved forwards, put a hand on the boy's shoulder, and gently pulled him back. Turning to Queen Nukeander and looking her in the eye, the King said, "Call him off!"

The Black Queen gathered herself, but instead of speaking she spat at Walterbald's feet.

"Very well," said Walterbald, and he turned to face Braggardio. "You would go through with this?" For Walterbald knew that Braggardio had grounds to challenge Stormy. But this was his daughter they were talking about.

"You would pit your superior strength and skill as a soldier against a girl of thirteen winters ... and be ridiculed throughout the west?" said the King.

"Horrible, horrible man," Gigi wailed.

The psykologicks was, however, lost on Braggardio. Having been eagerly thrust into the shoes of leader for the mighty Oosarian Army overnight, and then to have the imperial dream snatched away by a bunch of giggling baboons, was all too much. Some of the tendons that connected his thinking to reality had been severed. His brain rationalized it thus: *If he could not own Morainia, he would not be denied his revenge.*

"Stand aside, King, or I will kill you, too."

Walterbald, of course, did not budge.

Stormy ran forward screaming. She pushed at her father and still he did not budge. Then turning quickly she grabbed the hatchet from Gwynmerelda's hands, wheeled around and struck at Braggardio.

Braggardio laughed, but even in his twisted mirth his reflexes kicked into action. He easily deflected the blow with his broadsword. Stormy turned to strike again, and once again Braggardio effortlessly parried the blow.

Stormy knew how to wield a sword and an axe, and she could probably out-fence you or me. But pitted against a man trained in combat and in his physical prime, it was a battle she could never win.

Stormy spun around again, keeping the hatchet low. In the whirl of micro-moments she saw her father, Gwynmerelda, her grandparents, Geraldo. Her eyes flashed by Fred, and she saw The Fool running towards Eagle Cave. Then the thought hit her. She should do what she was good at. So, she ran. She ran to the river.

Stormy knew how to run. It was her Cliff Scout training. She could run up the Falls Road without having to stop for a break. She had run up much higher mountains in her dreams. She could also run downhill, steep downhill, and across very rough terrain, which she did now. Even carrying her mother's hatchet, she was as sure-footed as a mountain goat skipping across a boulder-strewn beach as she neared the water.

She had a head start ... the Prince was handicapped by armor ... if she could just ...

The screams of the crowd and the sounds of her pursuer merged into the crashing roar of Bald River Falls. The water's edge.

Don't look, she thought. Don't look back and don't look over the Falls. One false move, one wrong foot on the wet river stones, and she would be swept away. She slowed, but ran on. It appeared to the crowd on the rise behind her that she was walking on water.

The stepping-stones were only visible during high summer. It was not yet high summer, but it was not far off.

The night tales told of how the stepping-stones had been put there by Alexena, the Goddess of Rock. In the stories, Alexena enticed young men with her song, her beauty and promises of fame and longevity, to their inevitable deaths. Many had tried to cross, but the whisper of the Goddess in their ears became the roar of the crashing waters that swept them away.

Only one had ever successfully crossed the river. The giant Ohgerman. Ohgerman however, was intent on stealing Alexena's treasures and she had slain him with catapult and rocks. If only Stormy had a catapult with her now. She would instead have to use her wits.

It was all she had.

In the previous summer, Stormy had taken turns with Fred and some of the other Cliff Scouts, skipping out across the dry rocks to the thirteenth rock, just short of the mid-point of the river. Then it was theoretically possible to cross the whole way, but no one did, for the rocks in the middle were so close to the fall's edge, and the sound so mesmerizing, that no one dared.

It was July now, and high summer would not come until another moon. Still, Stormy could see those smooth white stones beneath her feet, just under the water. A fingernail deep, a first knuckle deep, and then as she strode out across the river, a second knuckle below surface. She felt the inexorable tug and drag of the river.

While the waters were deceptively clear this side of the Falls, they were as deep as a man was tall. The closer the rock path veered to the edge of the Falls, the deeper the water covering them became. It was in truth impossible to cross—even without the psykologickal fear of being swept over the edge.

Nine stones out into the water meant she was considerably closer to the edge of the Falls than she was to the bank. Stormy halted, the irresistible current now buffeting her ankles. Gasping for breath, she turned and saw Braggardio step from the bank onto the first of the submerged stones.

She could see the hate in his face, and she could see the apprehension creeping across his brow. Braggardio cautiously made his way on to the third rock. More cautiously still, he made his way across the next three rocks, wavering on the last, as his lead foot slipped a finger-length under the water.

He regained his footing, but as a man six and a half feet tall, his center of balance made him a mite more unstable than Stormy. It isn't always best to be biggest.

"Such a sweet pretty thing, but you will die, Princess," shouted the Prince, trying to regain the initiative. "Think your prophecy will save you now, girl?"

How did he know about the prophecy? Did everyone know about it? But Stormy forced herself to concentrate. She didn't think the prophecy would save her. She didn't know if she *could* be saved, and she had no idea what came next in her non-existent plan. Would that she were like her namesake Alexena, and could trick the man to his death.

Braggardio advanced one, two … more rocks with uncanny bravado and without hazard.

"Say your prayers, girl."

Stormy glanced over her left shoulder to the tenth rock and in the direction of the Falls. It was a little farther than a comfortable stride for her. Turning her body she leapt, and as her right foot landed she slid, crashing to her knee. Flailing and falling half forwards she crashed against the body of the rock, bringing her right arm down, and with it the hatchet that had been her mother's.

Mezzaculously, the hatchet blade found a fissure in the otherwise smooth rock. The force of Stormy's fall wedged the axe excaliberite into that rock, preventing her from being swept away. Grabbling with her left hand, she felt the blade sear into her fingers, but did not let go until she regained her balance and was able to pull herself up to standing.

Even above the din of the water, she could hear the screaming crowd now assembled on the bank. She looked up and saw Braggardio, advancing, laughing. She saw her father step out from the riverbank in pursuit of the Prince. She saw the blood dripping from her hand and felt dizzy with shock.

Only one empty rock now separated the Prince and Princess.

"One last miracle before you taste your reward, Princess!"

Stormy knew in her heart she had to end it. She could not risk Braggardio killing her father. She tugged at the hatchet with her good hand, but it was wedged solid. This was actually a good thing. Had Stormy swung the axe at The Prince as he landed on the rock next to hers, he would have been within striking distance to meet it with his sword. Again, that was a battle Stormy could never win.

As it was, she remained a finger-length out of reach as Braggardio swung his blade horizontally in the direction of Stormy's chest. Instinctively holding tight to the hatchet with her good hand, she was able to lean back that necessary finger length without losing her balance. If Braggardio leant forward the extra distance he would be the one toppling forwards.

"Come, Braggardio," shouted Stormy with a conviction she wasn't yet sure she felt. "Come taste the Prince Killer's kiss!"

Then she was, all of a sudden, sure. Quite sure.

Maybe she was possessed by Alexena the Goddess of Rock?

Alexandra Stormybald Wilson held out her bloody arm taunting Braggardio ... and withdrew it double speed, as he swiped again, wobbling dangerously.

"Strumpet! Whorlet! I can wait until you bleed to death."

And then Walterbald, sword drawn, was shouting behind him, and the Prince wheeled to look. He could spear the girl with his sword, but then he'd be defenseless against a bereaved king. End it now, he thought.

He turned back towards Stormy, and she saw the look in his eyes.

She could hear her father shouting, but dared not look. She flicked her left wrist theatrically, and droplets of her blood flecked Braggardio's face.

"Taste the blood of the Prince Killer," she screamed, and the scream filled the whole valley, drowning out the crashing of the waters, as Braggardio leapt at her, and they both plunged into the water.

Cold! Cold! Cold! The water stung her bloodied hand. Like cells dividing, fear replicated itself into a whole body panic. Where everything else was relentlessly fluid, Prince and Princess desperately clutched at each other. Then they crashed over the precipice, and Stormy saw black.

Braggardio's clinch relaxed and fell away, but as the shadow filled her senses she felt a new vice-like grip. Death's bony fingers and opposable thumb closed about her waist to squeeze the last breath from her, and then … and then—for shockingly there was an *and then*—the falling felt like soaring. Like when your hands are so cold with overexposure to ice they burn. What new kind of pain was this?

Instead of water crushing her, she felt the air rushing against her face, but still the tightening constriction around her stomach. Stormy felt that her eyes wanted to open, but she dared not let them. It had only now occurred to her that the torments that awaited the Prince Killer in death would be far worse than those of the world she was leaving behind. And then, another *and then* …

"An uncomfortably close, and unorthodox call, if I do say so myself," croaked The Gricklegrack.

Stormy opened her eyes for a second, saw the mighty talon that gripped her waist and the black, black feathers of Emmeur's belly, and promptly fainted ...

Far, far below, on the bow of the first longship—curiously separated from the other eight ships by the upended wreck of Toromos's ship—two Oosarian guards, Rosenstern and Guildenkrantz, were mesmerized by the huge black raven soaring above the falls. Wheeling majestically and to all appearances playfully, it had dived at the cascading waterfalls, as if taking a shower.

"Well, I'll be damned. Looks like he's got a fish!" said Guildenkrantz.

"Maybe an eel," replied Rosenstern. "Or one of them nymphemons they have up north."

"You don't see that every day," remarked Guildenkrantz.

"No, you don't. Whatever it was," said his comrade.

They were silent for a moment and then Guildenkrantz idly began tossing an Oosarian coin. "Nukeander or Merm?"

"Merm," replied Rosenstern.

"Merm it is," said Guildenkrantz.

"Yeh, but bloody well look at that. That ain't no mermangel," said Rosenstern as he rushed to the bow. They both saw a body floating towards the flat waters where the ships were moored.

"Should we fish him out?"

"Better had. If we know what's good for us."

After some commotion and with the help of the natural eddy which did most of the work in bringing the corpse to them, Guildenkrantz rolled the body over in the water with a pole.

"Wangus Corpus!" breathed Rosenstern as the stricken face broke the surface.

"Braggardio!" hissed a stunned Guildenkrantz

The landscape was no longer black, but Stormy found herself drifting between thoughts, which like the tentacles of a giant anemone wanted to ensnare her. She flicked her tail, her Mermangel's tail, and sped away. She saw the sun beckoning above and tasted the air as she broke the surface, flexing her wings and taking flight. The thoughts that chased her turned into winged harpies with the faces of people she knew. Everyone was barking questions at her: Queen Nukeander promised to hunt Stormy all her days. Rogerley Bishop, the rogue wangodmatist, asked if she was looking forward to eternal volcanemonic hell? Fred was riding a white donkey asking her to marry him. Her grandmothers were already arranging the wedding. Gwynmerelda wanted Stormy to tidy her bedroom. Stormy could not believe this last insult. *After what I've been through,* she wanted to say.

The Witch in the Ditch was saying "I told you so. I said Three Dead Princes and there are: Oooh let me count. One, Two, Three!" The Witch was drowned out by the gigglanths, merging into the laughing Giggle Monkeys of her dreams.

Glamour was telling The Witch to shut up, and Stormy wanted to go with her. But first she had to find her father. All she had wanted to do from the beginning was be with her father. Stormy saw The Fool and said: "Have you seen my dad?"

The Fool grimaced and nodded, indicating The Princess look behind her.

There was the cave, and there in the mouth of the cave was the giant black horned Cat saying:

"Well?"

"Well what?" said Stormy impatiently.

"Have you got it?"

"For a cat that speaks, you are mightily dense. Open your eyes. Look around you!"

The Cat looked around and smiled a Lancashire smile.

And then, where the Cat and the cave had been, there was a woman and a garden. She was bent, rooting some rose cuttings, but turned and stood as if Stormy had disturbed her. She dropped her metal trowel, and Stormy saw the woman's mud-stained fingers. Then the woman opened her arms, inviting her daughter's embrace, and Stormy hugged her mother Ursula.

"Alexandra Stormybald. You have all the time in the world ahead of you" Ursula said, and kissed Stormy on the forehead. She smiled at her daughter and said "I love you." Stormy's heart melted and then her mother said, "And now you can open *your* eyes."

Stormy had only been unconscious for a few moments before The Gricklegrack had landed, and a few moments afterward. But she was momentarily blinded by the sunshine and overwhelmed by the noise of everyone around her, flapping, cooing, and cheering the miracle. The fingers of her left hand seared with pain, but she could feel that someone had bandaged them. Even before her senses came into true focus, she knew that she was being cradled in her father's arms.

"I love you," said her father.

"I love you too," said Stormy and she wept as her dad helped her up.

She could hear The Fool shouting "Give her room, she needs air!" She could hear Zilpher and Gigi swooning with relief and the hubbub of the crowd beyond.

And then she felt Gwynmerelda move to embrace her husband and she saw the happiest expression on her dad's face that she could ever remember.

Stormy found herself smothered between King and Queen. It did not matter that the metal of the Morainian mountains of Gwynmerelda's breastplate dug into her back. For it was also the happiest feeling of the Princess's life. The three of them stood, royally grand, but only sort-of-like a royal family. For moments upon moments they held each other and let the good tears roll.

Chapter 21
THE RIDDLE OF THE EGG

Happily ever after? In the days that followed, Stormy simply wanted to disappear into the familiar surroundings of Bald Mountain Castle. She was happy to spend time doing very ordinary things. She was happy to eat food and help make it, and was even glad to be told off by Gwynmerelda for not tidying her room.

The battles were over and the war was avoided for now. But along with the happiness came some darkness. Her mind was bombarded with questions, some real, some imagined— questions that seemed to demand answers she did not wish to confront.

She was *the* Prince Killer of Andean legend? Was she cursed by Queen Nukeander? Were there other princes who would seek revenge for their brothers' deaths? Would someone track her down one day?

Would someone come back and try to take Morainia all over again? Would she be forced to marry some other Prince to avoid it? But no one would ever want to marry her, except Fred, and she didn't want to get married anyway!

Stormy got nervous one day when she woke for breakfast, and her dad was already up and away in the fields helping re-jig some irrigation channel. He was only a short walk away, but she could not eat breakfast before she saw him. Her nightmares and dreams would take a long time to heal. Some would never disappear.

But it was not all bad. She also had a vague memory from a dream that she should strive to be patient, to try to allow her mind to heal as her fingers would. The scars would remain, but the worst of the pain would recede, if she could but let go of it.

Stormy remembered the feeling of the dream one morning while she sat in the sun in the castle garden, smelling the roses which Ursula had first cultivated. Her grandfather Jakerbald had offered to teach her how to tend the roses, and they began an experiment in cross-kinking two different varieties. Stormy found it to be the most relaxing thing in the world during those days.

When her father suggested that he head back up north, as she knew he inevitably would, Stormy panicked and burst into tears. Stormy had been reluctant to leave the grounds of the castle, even to go the short distance into town. The day she tried to go to the library with Gwynmerelda escorting her, they bumped into Fred. Stormy panicked and ran home.

As well as not wanting to leave home, she felt trapped. She could never leave Morainia, for she would surely be arrested on sight—as she nearly had been that time in the Grackle Tavern. Her father had assured her this fear was nonsense, for as word travelled across the northern kingdoms of how the Oosarians had tried to force designs upon Morainia, there was little popular sympathy for the southern cause. Moreover, no authority would dare take action against the legendary Stormy of Morainia, or the Prince Killer as she was popularly known, for fear there would be a mass uprising such as had never been seen.

Stormy really did not like being treated as a hero. She did not feel like a hero, and though she would, over a long time, learn to live with it, it was a feeling she never felt entirely comfortable with in all her later adventures.

Walterbald, of course, promised his daughter that he would never make the journey north without her. "One adventure at her time," he had said.

And so Stormy was mostly happy to travel up north again by slow donkey, happy to miss the crowds of Archmotherfest, and happy to embrace the restorative powers of the Morainian summer. Best of all was the complete and utter luxury of having her father in her sight every day before sleep, and seeing his beaming face again when she woke up.

Jakerbald was with them on the journey. He had told Stormy not to worry about their roses, for both Zilpher and Gwynmerelda were more than capable horticulturalists. The Fool, who had been practicing his craft at the Andean encampment, was traveling with General Ghazali and would meet them there.

Thus a little over four weeks (as the Andeans called their artificial groupings of seven day periods) after the Battle of Bald River Falls, The Gricklegrack made good on his promise.

There at The Witch in the Ditch's cabin was assembled in a rag-bag order: The Witch of course, and Glamour her daughter; three generations of the Wilsons—Jakerbald, Walterbald, and Stormybald; The Fool, and General Ghazali of Andea; and, of course, Emmeur the Great Bird, who was feeling much more himself after his wounds had healed.

In the warm sun of high summer they pondered the strange egg before them. They pondered and pondered, and then Ghazali suddenly said, "Maybe it's a screw-top?" laughing as he said it.

The others looked at him bemused.

Spitting into his palms and then rubbing his hands together vigorously, Ghazali addressed the egg. Grappling it between his knees, he used his whole upper body to try and get some purchase on the dull, but still slick thing. He somehow managed to get a grip with the flats of his hands, above the perfect hairline crack that ran horizontally around the toppermost portion of the egg. He wrestled with the bit one would slice off the top of a soft-boiled egg, to enable the dunking of toast soldiers into a runny yolk.

He laughed as he felt some movement, wrestled some more, and gingerly began to unscrew the lid of the egg. To the amazement and applause of those gathered around, he lifted the lid away and took a bow.

Walterbald was the first into action, busily examining the thread around the lip of the lid with fascination. Inlaid into the lid were the numbers "323/1000." Those would eventually tell future examiners that it was one of a series. And then there were words, saying that this particular egg came from "West Yorkshire."

Jakerbald was about to peer into the egg itself when a never-before-heard beeping noise sounded.

The Witch shrieked with trepidation. Ghazali laughed,

of course. There was a sort-of-communal "*hmmm*" of intense curiosity from the others.

Though none knew it then, once the egg was open, the warm rays of the summer sun had struck the black panel that was inside it, triggering a whirring of invisible moving parts.

All gathered and watched in stunned silence, as a strange thing—the herald of yet stranger things to come, happened. Along an invisible vertical joint, the egg opened like a book would. But this, of course, was like no book anyone present had ever seen.

Constructed of some combination of plastics, stainless steel, titanium, and other ancient alloys, the egg had been specifically designed to withstand the centuries. Inset to a thumbnail's depth inside the right half of the egg was an oblong panel of opaque silver-gray material. The silver screen remained dull and lifeless.

The left-hand half of the egg seemed to be a compartment, made up of three small drawers. Above these at the top were three smaller black panels, each the size of a comb. It was these that drew the attention first, as one after the other they burst into life.

"By the beard of Alchemedes, tis magickery beyond anything," whispered Glamour as her mother cowered behind her, incanting unintelligible protective spells.

"Tis lightning captured in a box!" wailed the Fool, and in this he was closer to the truth than he could have known. The technology of the mid-to-late twenty-first century had been based upon that of leaves. The black panels at the top of the egg absorbed solar energy and mimicked photosynthesis, converting sunlight into the molecules that powered the hidden veins, branches, and roots within the egg. All with the perfect economy of a tree.

From left to right, red lightning bug numbers began to glare in the tiny boxes, changing numbers—numbers with meaning. The digital clock seemed almost comprehensible to Ghazali, beginning at zero, and counting off: 0.01. ... 0.02. ... 0.03. ... like extended heartbeats.

"Seconds," marveled Ghazali. "And watch!" As the count hit sixty, the zero changed to a one, and the count to sixty began again.

"Tis the ways of the Ancient Ones. A beautiful minute," he exclaimed with a laugh.

The central of the small screens was illuminated with ten zeroes and remained unchanging, but it was the right-hand screen that was most incomprehensible. The numbers flashed rapidly, like the egg was being scrambled to come up with the answer to an intractable problem.

And then the clock stopped on the number 164,092.

"Gadzillions!" said Jakerbald.

"Could it be that it has counted the number of ... the number of summers since ... since this machine was made?" suggested Walterbald looking at Ghazali.

Ghazali nodded and laughed. "Anything seems possible now!"

Nothing else unusual happened from within the egg itself for a long time. Over fifty minutes passed, according to the

clock, but in reality time flew by. During that interim, led by Walterbald, the travelers very cautiously opened each of the three drawers, one by one.

The first contained a book. A book in the same form that Stormy would have handled when she helped out at Morainia library. The book's pages were made of wafer thin plastic, which rustled as the King leafed through it.

"Dic-ti-on-A-ree," he announced trying to pronounce the strange word on the cover, and he handed the book to Stormy. She held the strange fabric and sat down with Glamour as she opened its pages. It was a book of mostly strange words and a few that seemed almost familiar. Incredibly, the language, though it possessed only twenty-six letters, was the same one she knew. There were only a few words on each page, and pictures.

"It's a children's book," she announced. Sure enough, many of the words were accompanied by finely detailed outline drawings.

Walterbald continued leading the investigations into the other two drawers. The second drawer contained a sheaf of plastics. Walterbald delicately took the top sheet and passed it on, and then the next and the next. They were very familiar looking children's drawings. Houses, people, trees, animals, the sun like a golden star in a blue sky. One even had a black bird sat in a tree. The bird was not unlike Emmeur's cousins of the raven world.

Another drawing had a strange flying creature with smiling people somehow inside it. It seemed featherless, with smooth wings. Walterbald looked at Emmeur, but neither could conceive what the creature in the drawing was.

The third drawer contained a dress made of some incredibly light and shiny fabric. The dress was red, but twinkled in the sunlight like crystallized frost in a full moon. There was a pair of flat shoes, which again were constructed of unusual materials. The shoes were what we would call a pair of sneakers. There was also a cheap plastic tiara.

Glamour nudged Stormy. "Well, go on! Try it on, girl!"

Walterbald held out the dress for his daughter and went back to examining the egg with the other scientics.

"Look," she cried, reading the label inside the back of the neckline. "It has my name in it. Sort of? It's called Stormskin!"

"I don't think it would offer much protection in a storm," said Glamour laughing.

The Princess stripped down to her knickers with none of the modesty of the twenty-first century from where the garb came, and pulled the sleeveless dress over her head. It hugged her teenage figure, went well with her boots, and felt as if it became part of her skin. As if she were almost wearing nothing.

Glamour cooed as she fixed the tiara in Stormy's hair, and then The Witch issued a baleful cry

"Tis possessed."

And surely, as the fabric absorbed some of Stormy's body heat it changed color in waves from reds, to purples, to aquamarines. The changing colors swirled, toppling over each other as the Princess moved.

"Look, look," called Emmeur. "There is even more wonder

here."

The silver screen in the right hand of the egg had suddenly blinked once, and then sputtered with a magnesium white flash. All eyes turned to watch the screen.

"*Urrgghh!*" The Fool sputtered aghast, peering intently as the screen came to life. They all gathered to watch the first moving pictures seen on Earth for, oh, about 162,000 years.

The comrades were transfixed. Some seventh sense somehow told them that this wondrous time capsule was benign, and in that they were right.

A group of seven children filled the screen: four girls and three boys. They wore very odd clothing, Stormy remembered thinking later. Most of them looked to be about Stormy's age, maybe some eleven-summer-olds, but mostly twelve or thirteen, she guessed, apart from a smaller girl in the front with long blond hair who was maybe nine.

They were all waving, laughing, saying hello, and cheering. And then on cue, they began singing in strange accents:

> *We do say ta for the humble Atom,*
> *From which all things are made.*
> *We do say ta for our universe,*
> *And our home, the Milky Way.*
> *We do say ta for planet Earth,*
> *And its relation to the Sun.*
> *We do say ta for the lucky place,*
> *We find ourselves in.*

We do say ta for the atmosphere,
Which warms us through and through.
We do say ta for the spark of life,
From which all beings grew.
We do say ta for evolution,
For giving us a lucky break.
We do say ta for the adaptation,
So that we can communicate.

We do say ta for our imagination,
And dreams that still surprise us.
We do say ta for ingenuity,
And let us use it wisely.
And though our life is in many ways brief,
Let our time be full of wonder ... aahh.
And if any should ever hear this rhyme,
Then we do say ta ... and hello ... and hurrah.

The children continued smiling and waving, but the younger girl at the end burst into tears, hid her face and turned away. A couple of the other children looked uncomfortable.

Then the shadow of a hand appeared in front of the group, blocking out the screen somewhat. One of the children said "Is that it, Mister Holdsworth?" An unseen man's voice said: "That were great!"

The screen went blank and resumed its silver lifeless pallor.

Those gathered by The Witch in the Ditch's cabin were all silent for a good while. As well as being astounded by this magickery, Stormy was overwhelmed by the human emotion therein. Maybe because they were children, to all appearance not unlike herself. The emotion was contagious, and as she looked at Glamour, they both saw the tears in each others' eyes.

It was The Fool who spoke first in a low whisper. "Holy 'scremis!"

"Poor little Devils. Elf faeries trapped in the egg for all eternity," barked The Witch in the Ditch.

It seemed like a long time before anyone spoke again, though it was only twenty-three seconds by the firebug clock.

And then a voice broke the silence ... it was the voice of a woman who had lived all those thousands of years ago: "At the third stroke it will be One o'clock precisely ... *beep beep beep.*" And the first clock on the egg registered the first hour as having passed.

"What a treasure box!" said Walterbald.

"But what does it all mean?" asked Stormy.

"I think—and it's only a theory," said Walterbald, "it's like a children's scrapbook from a long time ago. It means, and I am only making a first educated guess, that there were intelligent people, like ourselves, before the dark times. I would hazard a guess, that they maybe knew the dark times were coming, and they would probably not survive them. Hence they made this," and he paused before he said the word, "Time—egg."

Stormy looked sad, and her dress shimmered a somber green to match. She thought of the smallest girl inside the egg, crying after the children's song. Stormy went to hug her father.

"Well, for us, dear Alex," Walterbald said, "the same as we eat your granddad's chicken eggs for strength, this egg will be food for our brains every time we take in its wonders."

Looking into her father's eyes, Stormy suddenly felt very glad to be alive. Though the game of Rock, Shadows, Wonder, had not yet been invented, she knew in that moment—if we let it, wonder conquers darkness every time.

Author's Response

"WHY AN ANARCHIST FAIRY TALE?"

> No period of history could better illustrate
> the constructive powers of the popular
> masses than the tenth and eleventh centuries,
> when the fortified villages and marketplaces,
> representing so many "oases amidst the
> feudal forest," began to free themselves from
> their lord's yoke, and slowly elaborated the
> future city organization: but, unhappily, this
> is a period about which historical information
> is especially scarce; we know the results, but
> little has reached us about the means by which
> they were achieved.
>
> —Peter Kropotkin
> *"Mutual Aid – A Factor in Evolution"(1902)*

An anarchist fairytale may seem a contradiction in terms. Kings and queens, princes and princesses, serving girls and slaves? You have met them all in these pages. You found some of the regular doses of violence and struggle which survival compels, but also some fine moments of outstanding cooperation between people—and between species.

These ideas are not made up. There are many instances of symbiotic behavior between animal species in the nature we know. As, Bernd Heinrich points out, the raven evolved with the wolf, hence its nickname of wolf-bird. Ravens will, quite unbelievably, shy away from animal corpses—food just sitting there waiting to be eaten—to the point of not eating it, unless wolves (or surrogate wolves) are present. Ravens, who cannot slice up deer carcasses with their beaks, let the wolves do the hard work and then take their share. But why don't the wolves just eat the ravens as a tasty hors d'oeuvre? Because wolves learned that if the ravens behave in a particular way, they have, with the advantage of their aerial vision, spotted real food waiting to be eaten in the immediate environs.

In our world, though it is very different in some ways to Stormy's, there are real kings and queens, and nation states engaged in empire-building wars. There are rulers bent on suppressing those who resist their power. But there are also many exceptions to this, that the history of power neglects to mention. The "exceptions" to deadly competition or top-down domination involve another kind of power. And this power of cooperation between people is sometimes called "anarchism."

There was an actual anarchist prince in old Russia, called Peter Kropotkin. And contrary to the stereotyped image of the black-cloaked, bomb-throwing anarchist, Kropotkin was a rational, articulate thinker. He saw in the wider world around him some of the quintessential elements of non-hierarchical anarchist society. He developed a theory of the human tendency toward cooperation, or *mutual aid* as he called it, rooted not in wishful thinking, but in observable science.

Building on Russian scientific thought of his day, Kropotkin wrote a book called *Mutual Aid: A Factor in Evolution (1902).*

The book gave a scientifically respectable theory that for many species, cooperation, or mutual aid, was as much a part of survival for the species as a group, as the survival of the fittest was for the individual. In other words, the individual benefited from the cooperation of the group, whereas the group did not necessarily benefit from the elevation of the individual.

Kropotkin based his theories on observations of animals and indigenous peoples he made while working as a geographer and zoologist, during scientific expeditions in Siberia and Manchuria. He found human societies that were not all as competitive, as compared to the dangerously competitive nations of his own Western Europe of the late nineteenth century.

Contemporary scientists are still arguing over the fine details of how social and natural evolution works, and how this is different for each particular species. But present day evolutionists are finding that much of the general sense of Kropotkin's ideas was on track. For example, evolutionary scientists E. O. Wilson and D. S. Wilson explain,

> Hunter-gatherer societies are fiercely egalitarian. Meat is scrupulously shared; aspiring alpha males are put in their place; and self-serving behaviors are censured. Unable to succeed at each other's expense, members of hunter-gatherer groups succeed primarily by teamwork. (2008)

In evolutionary terms, we are all "modern humans," descended from those who first walked out of a gorge in Africa and spread across the world. As a species, we are approximately 150,000 years old, and until the dawn of agriculture 13,000 years ago, we were all hunter-gatherers. In other words, for most of our existence we lived co-operatively. And many of us today yearn for community in some form.

With Morainia, I am speculating as to where the line is between egalitarian bands of fifty or a hundred hunter-gatherers, and the sedentary, farming-based societies of a few thousand people which succumbed to hierarchical feudalism. For surely such a change did not happen overnight?

Kropotkin argued against the Social Darwinism of his own time, which advanced the idea that rich people deserved to be rich because they were fitter in evolutionary terms than poor people. Such warped misrepresentations of Darwin's theory would be used by Hitler, as justification for the master race of Nazi Germany, and a global war for the survival of only the fittest.

Some of the recently discovered evidence that humans evolved to co-operate has been staring us in the face on a daily basis. For example, David Sloan Wilson explains the unique adaptation of humans—among the other ninty-two of their primate cousins studied—of having exposed bright eye-whites (sclera). In contrast, chimpanzees, bonobos, gorillas, orangutans et al., along with most other mammals, have mostly concealed or darker-pigmented sclera. The darker sclera, or *nature's sunglasses,* evolved partly due to the general need of animals in the wild for camouflage to survive. But they also served a need of hierarchical ape society, to conceal information from rivals in their own group.

In stark contrast, humans are literally born to attract each other's attention by eye contact. The naturally selected exposed eye-white draws us into the window of the soul. Eye contact is how a baby learns about itself from its mother; it is the means by which we fall in love; and it is the basis of our trying to appeal to someone's better judgment in times of crisis.

It does not take a trained scientist to notice that the very first thing animators do to humanize their cartoon animals into talking life, is to give them very visible eye-whites. The scientist would ask whether our closest relative in evolutionary history, Neanderthal Man, had exposed eye whites? And bone remains only tell us so much, and just as we have no idea what colors dinosaurs actually were, we know nothing of the Neanderthal eye. But at some point, hundreds of thousands of years ago, the human eye diverged from that of other primates, and the advantage in terms of survival, of being better-able to share information and co-operate, was spectacularly successful.

That humans evolved to be involved in parenting over a matter of years, rather than months or weeks, offers more evidence of mutual aid as a factor in evolution. How could a human baby ever live beyond a few hours were its parents, or substitute care-givers, not hard-wired to raise it through the years when it simply could not fend for itself? And beyond family cooperation, there would be no great cities, no great leaps in technology, no man on the moon, no titanium rod in my broken leg, no avoiding untold havoc wreaked by global warming, if humans had not discovered, and do not rediscover, our natural leaning towards mutual aid.

The mess the modern world finds itself in has been built upon the misappropriation of our cooperative nature.

Contemporary evolutionists say that when a society is too successful, and the surpluses from co-operating grow too great, then some individuals try to benefit at the expense of the group. A few will take the vertical fast route to power over others. And the grand view of history is littered with individuals who claimed superiority over society—by divine right, by force, or by entrenched privilege. These are the tyrannical kings and queens; the hypocritical priests and bishops; the dictators and corrupt politicians, who seem to fill our history books. And now we see a new wave of self-serving corporate bosses, animated with a similar sense of entitlement.

In the year 2010, few would disagree that we have lost our sense of balance with and within our planetary environment. Few would deny, that should we continue to hurtle down this road, there awaits a spectacular collapse, in some form, at some point. Perhaps the way we can avoid such a collapse is by rediscovering the evolutionary self that tends towards mutual aid: the self which makes us human.

You have just read a tale of a world that had collapsed. Some species survived, and some evolved, somehow managing to reinvent their lives from the bottom up, with whatever was closest at hand. Will they go on to make the same mistakes that we are making? There are kings and queens, monsters and all the rest ... it is a fairy tale after all ... But perhaps unlike many fairy tales, and more like life itself, there are also sprinklings of anarchy and mutual aid in the moments when needs must ...

Danbert Nobacon
Twisp, Washington

Acknowledgments

Many thanks to my wonderful editor and publisher, Tod Davies.

Alex Cox for imagining the characters in such a spectacular way. Mike Madrid for his tireless efforts in that universe called graphic design, which will always remain a mystery to me.

A toast to Charles Darwin, Jared Diamond, David Sloan Wilson, E.O. Wilson, Bernd Heinrich, Bill Bryson, Alan Weisman et al. for fomenting the dialogues in my head that made the world of this book seem sort-of-possible.

Thanks to the Banks Lake crew for entertaining the Gricklegrack.

And thanks to Laura Gunnip for her belief in me.

191

Glossary

adaman – the first man

adamonkey – common ancestor of humans and great apes

airgile – agility in the air

bepuzzled – puzzled

begoggled – dazzled

birch-barker – someone who gets the wrong idea, and barks up the wrong tree

birded – to be kept informed by message bird

blasfamy – blasphemy

blasfenemies – enemies, distinguished by a supposedly heretical nature

boggled – mind boggled

boggler – someone who sees but does not necessarily understand: a nosey boggler, nosey parker, nosey beggar

boggerworts – general term for warts, derived from boggarts who are prone to having warts

brainfryingly – the adrenalin rush of terrifying endeavor, such as downhill skiing or roller coaster riding

brethsisteren – brothers and sisters

celestion – a heavenly being, a god, or god-like creature

cessprince – derogatory term for a princess

changefigured – transfigured, transkinked, evolved

chittle-chattle – gossip

crizeymas – winter festival, sometimes called Iziemas

confuzzled – confused, bepuzzled

crookedy – crooked

devanimal – according to the wangodmatist way of thinking, the renegade animals who had caused the Wangod to curse earth with the dark times. Any creature or person heretical to wangodmatist ideas

earthrumble – earthquake

ennunced – enunciated

ensluicing – taming by cruel means

excaliberite – wedged like a sword in rock

flameringly – obvious, literally as noticeable as flames

fretter, frettered – to fret, did fret

gadzillion – an unimaginably large number

gatoriles – large lizard-like creature such as a crocodile

gigglanth – genus of laughing men and women

gigglanthropic – the quality of being gigglanthine
grabbled – grappled, wrestled.
gracklebrain – someone not quite with the program
graydark – the eerie three-quarter dark of the dust-filled skies
    during that cataclysm
grickles – shorthand for genus known as gricklegracks
gropple – grope
groppled – groped, molested
guffackling – guffawing, cackling
jekkler – a joke, particularly a rib-tickling joke
kero-lamps – kerosene lamps
kink/kinks – the mutant gene/genes that power evolution or
transkinkery – the process of evolution
kingdidates – candidates for election of king
lateen – someone in their late teens: usually an indication of
    a more worldly wise youth than what most would think
    of twenty-first century teenagers
loominated – illuminated by moonlight
magickery – magic, seemingly supernatural phenomena
man-to-man – male homosexual, gay-boy
marriage brokery – matchmaking, the business of arranging
    marriages
mechanagics – seemingly magical, but actually mechanical
memobird – a message bird
mezzaculously – miraculously
moonblood – menstrual blood, period
morningsun – east, or meaning directional right, towards the
    right

mothshark – huge mythical flying beast who brought people from the other side of the world

mysterhyme – riddle talk

nobadness – goodness

nymphemon – a she-demon of the river

pompiffery – ceremony, pomp

potstillery – brewhouse

prancer – one who prances about

pretendsuppose – make belief, a pretendsuppose story

probber – a priest or parson, a wangodmatist who teaches others in the ways of the Wangod. A professional missionary

probber's nosc – parson's nose, the rear end of a bird, anatomically a bird's anus

pumpeduppery – puffed up,

pumpery – extenuated tavern talk, regarding the fine, and to most people, the boring details of machinery

psykologicks – psychology

pyskosicks – dangerous sickness of the mind

quizzlcprink – upstart

redfish – salmon

regaliocol – royal protocol

romp-pomp-pum-paggle – street or bar-room theater

rumble-wave – tsunami, a giant wave

sagack – sage, guardian, chaperone

scarify – scare, frighten

schoolchilder – schoolchildren (plural)

schemagems – schemings, tactical plans, strategems

scientic – scientist
scientical – scientific
screek – schreech
skimble skamble – nonsense
skydynamics – aerodynamics
skolarshop – a workshop cum study
sledblastering – involuntary outburst as a result of high adrenalin activity
smakker – mouth, lips
smakobbed – gob-smacked
spasmering – convulsing, gripped by spasms
splinterendering – the cracking of wood as it caves in under pressure
sticklerish – quality of being a stickler for the rules
swaggerswanking – swashbuckling
ta – thanks
Tavernmizz – senior waitress in a pub, barmaid
thezzpians – theatrical types
Time Egg – a time capsule
transkinkery – the process of evolution
turkabird – a wild turkey
volcanemon – volcano, perceived by the western peoples to be enraged earth spirits
wan, wance – one, once
Wangod – the one god
wangodfearing – deeply religious
wangodknowswhere – the one God knows where
wangodmatist – believer in, or practitioner of, wangodmatism,

the worship of the Wangod to the exclusion of all others
wangodsakes – for godsakes
whoosh-shoosh – sound of rushing, air or water
whorlet – teenage or young whore, term of derision
wonderlook – a small but powerful telescope.
zizzerhither – hither-thither

DANBERT NOBACON, singer, songwriter, comedian, and "freak music legend," was a founding member of the anarchist punk rock band Chumbawamba.
He loves children and animals.

This is his first book.

ALEX COX is better known for his filmmaking skills.
He loves monsters.